HEIR HEART

Revenge of the Lost Inheritance

LANA TORIZI

Lana Torizi
Heir Heart: Revenge of the Lost Inheritance

Published by BooxAi
ISBN: 978-965-578-802-0

CHAPTER 1

Veronica's hand flew to her chest, her fingers trembling as an invisible weight pressed down against her. The classroom, once buzzing with energy, spun into a dizzying blur. She could hear the echo of a student's question, the words stretched and gargled, as if underwater.

As the darkness clawed in, a familiar voice whispered through the chaos - a voice that belonged to a world beyond; it was her father who had left years ago. Each blackout had brought his words closer, a message shrouded in the mystery of the afterlife.

Consciousness returned as a jolt, the sterile lights of a hospital corridor piercing Veronica's eyes. The rhythmic clicking of the gurney's wheels on the linoleum floor anchored her back to reality. But the reality was that these were no ordinary migraines; they were a bridge to something beyond, something both terrifying and alluring.

Her father's messages were becoming clearer, and more urgent. Lying there, the murmurs of nurses and the beep of machines fading into a distant symphony, Veronica knew a decision loomed over her. She could no longer shield her students, or herself, from the unknown dangers of these episodes. The resignation was inevitable, but it was no longer about the job she was leaving behind, but rather about the gateway to uncovering a truth beyond the shadowy corners of her mind about her father that summoned from the supernatural.

When her sons arrived at the hospital to persuade her to step down, she needed little convincing. However, without her income, paying the monthly mortgage would be impossible. She would have to sell the house. And since none of her sons offered to take her in, she faced some difficult choices: a low-budget trailer home or a chintzy apartment.

Was she really this desperate? She yearned for something better. A nostalgic image of her childhood home—a beautiful Spanish white stucco hacienda with a red tile roof, beamed ceilings, and a room featuring a balcony—flashed before her eyes. Anger and resentment welled up within her as she remembered how her sister Karina had sold their childhood home to pay off her gambling debts. How could she have let it go for such a paltry sum? The house was now worth double!

Could she settle for a trailer home in her retirement, her so-called golden years? But then, inspiration struck. Veronica was her father's daughter, after all. She recalled that he had left her a beach house in Mexico, which her sister had been maintaining because Veronica couldn't afford the upkeep on her miniscule Arizona teacher's salary. That house could be her ideal retirement home, far exceeding any affordable options in Phoenix. She owned it outright; her only financial obligations would be taxes and a trust paid to the Mexican government, along with utilities.

Mexico, with its serene beaches and tranquil sunsets, offered a beautiful haven in which to spend her golden years. And so, amidst the chaos of her present, Veronica found hope, painted in the warm colors of sandy browns, ocean greens, and sky blues, guiding her toward a peaceful future.

"But, Mom, are you sure you can manage life alone in Mexico? Is it going to be safe down there?" her eldest son, Joseph, asked.

"There's only one way to find out," Veronica replied.

Within a week, she had turned over her Phoenix house to the

bank due to mounting debts. Unable to afford the $3,000 for a moving truck, her sons took on the task of packing her belongings, filled their cars to the brim, and formed a caravan to transport her to her Mexican home. Unable to afford the $3,000 for a moving truck, her sons took on the task of packing her belongings. They filled their cars to the brim and formed a caravan to transport her to her Mexican home. They brought her paintings, clothes, jewelry, and an extensive collection of books—though no furniture, as the house was already furnished.

"Now, you boys know that I don't drink much, and I don't use drugs," Veronica reassured them.

"I've been a teacher all my life, so it's unlikely I'll get into trouble. I don't do wild, late-night, drunken parties, and I have my dogs to alert me if someone comes around. There's no need to worry about me."

"I also have the rental management company that makes my bill payments; they'll help me if I need anything."

Her sons unloaded their cars, filled with their mother's cherished items, carefully unpacking a 12 place setting of Portmeirion Botanic Garden China; a Spode Christmas China set; special gemstone pieces from the Tucson Gem and Mineral Show; her mother's own paintings; four Van Gogh reproductions; an assortment of collectibles; clothing for every season; and, most significantly, her favorite novels and poetry books amassed over years as an English teacher. With everything in place, her new residence abroad truly became her own, a distinct space reflecting her life and passions. When her sons' cars were empty, they returned to the United States, leaving Veronica in her new home. She felt a twinge of apprehension about her solitude in a foreign land, even though she had the means to stay connected with family and friends by phone. Yet this was her home, a space uniquely her own.

CHAPTER 2

Having risen from humble beginnings only to find herself back at square one, Veronica felt oddly at home. Despite attending private schools and living with the rich, she had never fully shed her sense of being an imposter. While she had developed a taste for finer things, she was far from a spoiled, little rich girl. Her father's frugality had remained with her, influencing her to seek out bargains. Although she and her children dressed impressively, thanks to carefully curated Goodwill finds, her inability to budget properly had led her through multiple bankruptcies and divorces. Yet, she had emerged unscathed, driven by an indomitable spirit, aided by her medication for depression, and not without hope for a better tomorrow.

At this time in her life, following her second divorce and with her children finally moving out, Veronica found herself alone. Well, not entirely—she still had Rudy and Riley, her loyal dogs, who she knew would protect her. Well, they were Corgis, not Rottweilers, so they would not win in a WWE cage match, but they'd put up a good fight.

She frequently pondered the sequence of choices that had brought her to this point. Alone in a foreign country, accompanied only by her dogs, she had never envisioned this in her later years.

Both her marriages had drained her finances, leaving her only with the Mexican beach house her parents had bequeathed to her—a beautiful property a block from the ocean, to which her sons had recently moved her.

Veronica, nearing 60, had always danced a precarious tango with finances and romantic liaisons. Two bankruptcies and the looming threat of a third had plagued her. Now, the time for her to carve her oath gleamed brightly before her. Deception of age ran through her veins; her other had been a master of it, effortlessly maintaining a façade of eternal youth. Having blurred the year on her driver's license with a strategically spilled drop of nail polish and securing sworn oaths of age-secrecy from her children, Veronica's preoccupation with maintaining her youthful image had never bothered her family. In fact, they embraced having an engaged, community-minded mother who encouraged participation in a plethora of activities, particularly those having to do with animals.

A soft spot for creatures had always nestled in Veronica's heart, granting her a voice that roared and barked with compassion for all beings great and small. From childhood, her parents had recognized her extraordinary connection with animals- horses grew serene under her guidance, and chickens miraculously laid more eggs in her soothing presence. The twinkle in her eye upon meeting a new creature sparked such joy that her parents implored her to consider veterinary school. But Veronica, moved by her passion for literature, a gift from her father, and, inevitably, by the whims of her heart where poetry and writing were concerned, chose English, and teaching, instead.

Her father, on the other hand, was an intellectual at heart, He had emphasized the importance of higher education and world exploration, cultivating their house to be a home filled with books that ranged from law cases and classic literature to cookbooks. This collection also included what he playfully termed his wife's "trashy novels"- which were, in fact, popular bestsellers._A true Renaissance Man, he had imparted the joy of lifelong learning to his children, filling their basement with bookshelves that were as diverse in genre as they were abundant in number.

The decision to write, then, felt like destiny to Veronica. She had pursued a career in teaching English and held a lifelong love for books; visiting libraries and bookstores felt like coming home. Now, as a new resident in a foreign land, she decided to channel her love of the written word differently—by starting a community newsletter.

Understanding the importance of fitting in, especially in a foreign country, she set out to connect with her new community. Her dogs could offer love but not real protection, so community ties were essential for her peace of mind. Taking the initiative, Veronica went door-to-door in her American-dominated neighborhood, soliciting articles, announcements, and affordable advertising for her bi-weekly newsletter.

Thus, the "Las Olas Times" was born. Initially sparse, the paper eventually grew to feature a variety of content, including local business news, personal interviews, art and writing contests, local recipes, tidal weather reports, and life events ranging from births to deaths. Over time, it swelled to 10-20 pages of community-contributed material, becoming an indispensable resource and a symbol of the interconnected lives of those who read it.

Starting her day with a cup of coffee, flavored with calorie-free creamer to mimic the luxury of a high-end coffee shop treat, Veronica settled in front of her computer to work on the next edition of her community newsletter. Once a victim of financial ruin, she had learned the value of frugality. The absence of her former husband, Joe, left her alone but also allowed her the freedom to take up a new endeavor. Although the newsletter began as a way to fill her time, it also satisfied her unspoken, nosy curiosity about the lives of her neighbors.

This endeavor gave her an excuse to interact with the community. Veronica learned about local happenings, whether it was the struggling business placing a "Going Out of Business" ad, or the heartbroken individual sharing a melancholy poem about a recent breakup. She even discovered where to find the best tamales during the holiday season. Funding the project out of her pocket, Veronica never expected any pushback—until she ran afoul of the homeowners' association for using the community name, "Las Olas," in her newsletter's title. To diffuse the situation, she renamed it "Rudy and Riley's Gazette," after her faithful dogs.

Wheeling a small wagon loaded with freshly printed newsletters, with Rudy and Riley trotting ahead, was the highlight of her delivery days. As she made her rounds, neighbors welcomed her into their homes, offering beverages and snacks along with additional stories for future newsletter editions. Her visits were generally pleasant, except for the inevitable HOA violation notice from Harry Hillsdale, the cantankerous president of the homeowners' association. Though he had initially objected to the newsletter, claiming it violated some unspecified board policy, he eventually relented. All he required was a disclaimer on the front page stating that the publication was "not endorsed by the Las Olas Community Property HOA." Of course, there were a few homes that Veronica chose to avoid. She would get a sudden migraine every time she and the dogs even tried to walk one step up their driveway. The old man with the ferocious Pitt bulls was not very pleasant, and she felt, what her son, Harry, called "her Spidey senses" get very up in arms every time she went near his house. He didn't want her there and she didn't want to be there. It was a mutual agreement.

The experience was a subtle reminder that even well-intentioned community projects could ruffle feathers, but for Veronica, it was all worth it. Every edition of "Rudy and Riley's Gazette" not only deepened her connection with her neighbors but also strengthened the community's bonds with each other.

Just down the street, Veronica met an intriguing couple: Dave and Irene Verducci. Dave had recently purchased their house for the surprising sum of $100,000 after the original owner had passed away. Not interested in living in Mexico, the owner's sister had decided to sell. Dave, hearing about the deal from the long-time caretaker of the property (an old construction buddy,) consulted his wife. Irene took one look at the property and instructed him to "Write a check immediately!" The couple had been married for 40 years; Dave was a contractor and Irene a secretary. Dave's philosophy for maintaining a happy marriage was to buy his wife a condo in another country. They had been visiting Mexico for years, and Dave credited the trips with strengthening their marital bond.

Soon, Irene and Veronica started spending time together, often visiting the Malecon for drinks and conversation. Veronica would bring her dog, Riley, for protection and companionship.

"Your dog seems incredibly in tune with you," Irene observed. "She stops when you stop and sits when you sit. What else can she do?"

"Believe it or not, Riley is something of a detective. She's helped me solve a few cases. It may sound crazy, but we have a unique understanding of each other," Veronica confided.

Irene chuckled. "Well, that does sound a bit 'far-fetched,' no pun intended. But I know dogs have heightened senses and perceptions that we don't fully understand. Perhaps you have a deeper connection with Riley than most people have with their pets. Let's leave it at that."

"Thanks for not thinking I'm crazy," said Veronica, relieved.

"I didn't say that," Irene replied. And they both broke into laughter, pouring just a little more cement into their already building friendship.

Along with creating a social life, everyday Veronica worked diligently to transform her father's aging property into a welcoming home. The cracked white stucco that adorned the exterior was a major concern. Not only did the cracks need filling and the walls painted, but the backyard wall also required an extension to give the dogs a secure area for "doing their business." She sought local expertise to tackle the problem.

Despite her limited Spanish, she relied on Google Translate for assistance. One contractor, Roberto Cameron, arrived in a flashy

Cadillac and quoted her 45,000 pesos—an exorbitant amount that felt like buying a new car. Then came Ernesto Moriega in his battered red pickup truck, who offered to do the job for just 30,000 pesos. Veronica hired him on the spot. Her father had always taught her to never trust the worker who came in his new car because that was what you would end up paying for.

"It also showed that he was used to getting his hands dirty and working hard. That's the kind of person you want working for you," her father would say.

Water supply was another pressing issue. To ensure a more consistent flow, Veronica invested in a 1,000-gallon tank. However, due to periodic water shortages in her part of town, she remained at the mercy of the city's supply. She discovered she could pay for additional water—at $100 per week to fill her tank—if she ever ran out. It was a costly backup plan but one that provided peace of mind. These were the realities of life in Puerto Bella.

CHAPTER 3

Though the prospect of a beautiful future now awaited her, Veronica couldn't shake off the nagging feeling of betrayal. She felt cheated by her sister, Karina, suspecting that she could have had more than just this house if Karina hadn't sold their family home. Veronica knew she needed to let go and move on, but her current home had only narrowly escaped her sister's grasp. For now, she harbored no warm feelings toward Karina.

"I'll only agree to turn the house over to you if you reimburse me $3,000 for this year's fees that I already paid," Karina said.

"Fine, I'll send the money via Zelle," Veronica replied.

"I could make you pay for all the renovations I did," Karina added, "but I guess that would be un-sisterly of me, wouldn't it?"

"You have stayed there many times over these sixteen years, didn't you? So, haven't those renovations benefited you as well? Besides, I have had to re-do all the shoddy workmanship of the plumbing system; update the water system, replace all the faucets; and start having monthly pest control to make sure that we aren't infested with bugs," Veronica countered.

Karina said nothing, accepted the $3000, and coldly walked away. She knew Veronica was right, and she didn't care about the property anymore; only what she could make from it.

Veronica had inherited her father's "do-it-yourself" work ethic. "No sense in paying someone else what you can fix yourself," he would often say. When she lived in the house on Helen Street after her first divorce, she was reminded of this saying every time the closet light automatically turned on when its door swung open.

Years later, even in her home in Mexico, traces of her father's peculiar taste could be seen everywhere. Non-matching light switch plates, some adorned with Mexican pottery designs and others featuring jumbled patterns like moose and bears, decorated the walls. The wrought-iron screen doors at the entrances also embodied his eclectic style: one was a fitting copper color with a sun ray design, while the other two—green with a palm tree and turtle, and blue with a bubble pattern—seemed out of place.

"Dad never settled for the ordinary," she mused to herself.

Thankfully, the house had since been updated with modern conveniences like air conditioning, cable, and Wi-Fi, dragging it into the 20th century. However, part of the allure of vacationing in Mexico had always been the opportunity to disconnect and unwind. In days past, the round table had been the gathering point for late-night games of Trivial Pursuit, a place where everyone focused on each other rather than their electronic devices.

Nowadays, with smartphones and television providing constant distractions, even she found herself giving in to the magnetic pull of a good movie—though not before she had counted the stars in the crisp, clear night sky.

One night, Veronica found herself in her usual spot, this time with her chair facing the dunes rather than the ocean. She gazed upwards at the cosmic display, jokingly crediting it to "yours truly, God," while her dogs listened attentively. As she moved, she realized she had left the balcony lights on. Pausing by the first lantern, she admired the intricate DeGrazia-style painting of a small child on its porcelain surface. She wondered if her mother, who had taken up painting in her later years, had crafted it.

Inspired, Veronica decided to conduct a "museum tour" of the outside lanterns. She examined each one in turn, speculating about the history behind them. With four lanterns to inspect, the activity consumed some time. However, as she reached the spot where the last lantern should have been, she found herself engulfed in darkness. Despite the heavenly light shown above, this corner of the house remained hauntingly dark, a space where a lantern would have been more than welcome as midnight approached.

Somewhat shaken, Veronica hurried back inside to grab her brightest flashlight. Anticipating a burnt-out bulb, she also took a fresh one and a small step ladder. When she shone the flashlight on the unlit lantern, she found it didn't match the others at all.

Naturally, this was her father's doing, and she should have known better. The lantern she found was an old, rickety construction made from driftwood and glass panels. It looked more like a bird feeder than a light fixture.

Moreover, it wasn't even wired for electricity; it contained an electric candle that ran on batteries. Perplexed about why her father would choose such a piece, Veronica decided she wouldn't keep the tacky item on her balcony. She unhooked the lantern, took it inside, and resolved to find a more aesthetically pleasing Talavera replacement the next day.

This was so like her father—a man molded by the past and the rigors of the Depression era. He'd never purchased a new car; in fact, her mother only bought a new car after he passed away. He'd taught Veronica how to drive using a '54 Peugeot with no speedometer, telling her to simply "go with the traffic." Frugal but not cheap, he'd always found ways to make do, often "jimmying" things to make them fit in his garage. Yet his thriftiness enabled all of his children to attend college, and nobody complained about his prudent lifestyle. At least not above a whisper.

Veronica recalled how they had bought their family home when she was six; it had been vandalized and the culprits had placed candles in the chandeliers. Unable to afford new carpeting, she and her mother painstakingly picked wax out of the existing carpet—a carpet that stayed in place until Veronica was in eleventh grade.

To most people, the lantern might appear to be mere

driftwood, the sort of object likely to feature in a DIY project guide someday. "One person's junk is another's treasure," or so her father believed. He saw value in everything and had a reason for most things he did. Veronica was sure he had placed that lantern intentionally, and its presence nagged at her.

The rusted ring on top was bent at an odd angle. The hinges of its door cried out in a creaking wail as if begging for a lubricating squirt of WD-40. And the glass? It was so marred by years of dirt, wind, and wear that it seemed beyond redemption. Viewing these flaws, she declared the lantern unworthy and consigned it to the pile of items to be burned in the back of the house.

Yet, this very lantern—the one she thought she had disposed of—mysteriously reappeared on her doorstep the next morning, clamped in Rudy's mouth. The dog was known for chewing things he shouldn't have, but even for Rudy, this was unusual behavior. He had shattered one of the lantern's lower glass panes and appeared to be trying to pry up the metal plate at its bottom, although unsuccessfully.

"Alright, Rudy, I see what you're getting at," Veronica said, taking the lantern from the dog's grasp. She headed for the "tool closet" her dad had set up, wading through its dusty, cobweb-laden shelves laden with cans of WD-40, dried-up paint, water bottles, bungee cords, and miscellaneous beach gear. Eventually, she found the screwdriver she needed. This task served as another reminder of the multitude of chores awaiting her; her father had certainly left her with her work cut out for her.

She brought the lantern and the screwdriver to the kitchen, the brightest room in the house. After about five minutes of prying, she removed the weakened frame and lifted the metal plate. Hidden beneath was a hollow chamber containing a key. She had almost thrown this away? Rudy seemed to know better. How did he know? What was truly happening here?

Clearly, something more significant was afoot—bigger than her, bigger than Rudy. Her father had orchestrated some hidden plan, and she had nearly missed it. From now on, she'd have to be more vigilant. This mystery was obviously meant for her alone, but she couldn't fathom what the key unlocked. The place had been rented out to various strangers over the years, and cleaners and workmen had come and gone freely while she and her sister were in the States. Moreover, her sister might have discovered this lantern and key and kept the secret for herself.

Yet, all these were mere possibilities. The undeniable fact remained that she alone had this key. She was the only one who would've noticed the lantern or understood her father's knack for improvising solutions. It seemed her father was leading her on a genuine treasure hunt to find the keyhole this key would unlock. Under the plate she had lifted, she also noticed an inscription: "Under the place where spiders dwell, only you can tell, where you and I can spell out the end."

The words left her intrigued and mystified. What did they mean? And where did spiders dwell in her house? What secret had her father hidden so intricately, and what role was she meant to play in unveiling it? The clues were right in front of her, but unraveling them would take some serious thought. Whatever it was, Veronica felt an electric charge of anticipation. A hidden chapter in her life was about to be written, and she was the one to pen it.

She knew exactly where spiders tended to dwell; she had recently had the area exterminated. It was the closet situated between the main house and the smaller studio of her Puerto Bella residence. She hadn't noticed any hidden doors or compartments there, but she also hadn't been actively searching for them, either. The quest her father set her upon was exceptionally secretive. To complete it, she needed to act when no one was likely to observe her. The early morning seemed the safest bet. Nighttime might be risky due to the shadowy activities some people engaged in, and she didn't relish the idea of rummaging around in that dark, spider-infested closet.

Though she lived alone, her integration into the community and the security measures put in place by her sons made solitude a rare commodity. Guards from the security service and representatives from the property management company routinely stopped by. She would have to proceed without arousing any suspicion. And she would need to find the mysterious keyhole quickly. Additionally, she decided it would be wise to repair the lantern, concealing the chamber where the key had been stowed, in case it had further significance.

Under the guise of modernizing her home, she headed to the *ferretería*, the local hardware store, to buy a doorbell. A recent medical evaluation revealed a 40% hearing loss in one ear, and she had been fitted with hearing aids. She often forgot to wear them because she could easily adjust the volume on her TV or phone. However, the devices were critical in public spaces, and she had been caught off guard more than once by quiet knocks at her door or even more disconcertingly, by people appearing at her window. Investing in a doorbell seemed like a practical step, especially for someone living alone.

Her initial concern was the electrical work involved in installing a doorbell. Fortunately, her dilemma was easily solved through technology. The local hardware store didn't have what she needed, but online platforms like Amazon Prime did. The best part was that she found a Ring Plug-in Adapter, eliminating the need for an electrician. She could even install Ring Chimes in less audible parts of the house, ensuring she would always hear when someone arrived. Thank God for YouTube tutorials!

The following morning, she woke up early. The world outside was eerily still, devoid of human activity. Perfect. She had to proceed quietly. After securing her front door, she ventured into the closet, flashlight in hand. After an extensive search, she found a tiny keyhole hidden near the base of the closet's rear wall. Tentatively, she inserted the key and turned it to the left—once, then twice. She heard a creak.

Suddenly, she lost her balance and fell backward. Regaining her composure, she noticed an opening had appeared, revealing stairs that led downward. It was a hidden chamber she had never known existed. She cautiously peeked out of the closet to ensure her clumsy fall and the mysterious door's creak had not attracted attention.

Secret-keeping wasn't her forte; she had never needed to be covert about anything before.

However, she felt it was crucial to honor her father's evident wish for secrecy. Who could she even confide in? Her sons were already concerned about her mental faculties, suspecting early signs of dementia. Keeping quiet, therefore, seemed not just possible but necessary. She was entrusted with something secret for a reason, and she was going to honor that trust.

As she descended the dark, stair-cased passageway, memories of her parents' old basement washed over her, accompanied by the musty scent of an aging water heater and timeworn books. Could her mother's Alzheimer's genes have manifested early? What was this place? It seemed like a time warp back to her childhood home, which was odd because that basement had been renovated years ago. She pinched herself, hoping to awaken from what must surely be a dream.

Illuminating her way with the flashlight, she noticed that the steps were uncanny replicas of those in her childhood home. They were even covered with carpet samples her mother had acquired from her work as an interior decorator. Her father had stapled these mismatched swatches, two to each step, creating a patchwork of eclectic but muted colors that dampened the sound of footsteps. And yet, despite its aesthetic shortcomings, the basement had been a magnet for guests.

"Oh, you have a basement? That's rare for Arizona. What's down there? Can I take a look?"

Her mother would invariably roll her eyes at the sight of those mismatched stairs and the cluttered space everyone seemed eager to explore. She'd divert visitors by offering tours of the rest of the house—every room a model of meticulous care and attention, thanks to the bi-weekly housekeeper. Yet, the basement was a no-go zone even for the maid. Tidying that space was a task no one dared to undertake.

Feeling as if she must be in a dream, she aimed her flashlight onto the walls in search of the familiar portraits: her father as a young man at Johns Hopkins, black and white snapshots of her family from before her birth, and a magnificent photo of her mother in her wedding dress—a picture she'd thought lost. When the beam of light found that last image, tears filled her eyes. She asked her sister about the photograph, but her sister said she had no idea of its whereabouts. It was an irreplaceable piece of memorabilia, and here it was, within arm's reach. Could she take it? She hesitated, mindful that even dreams have their rules. Just as she reached for the frame, a familiar voice rang out.

"I wouldn't do that if I were you."

"Dad? But you're—"

Sweat began to form on her brow, an early sign of an impending migraine. She felt lightheaded, and darkness swallowed her vision.

When she next opened her eyes, she found herself on the floor, a pillow under her head and a blanket draped over her.

"Hello. I apologize for the shock."

"But you died in 1986. I was right beside you the night before you passed away. So, have you been alive all this time, or are you just an 'undigested bit of beef,' a 'fragment of underdone potato' or a figment of my imagination?"

"Oh, I most certainly died. But I do love your *Christmas Carol* references! But for some unexplained reason, I was permitted to remain here, waiting for you to find me. I don't know how long I can stay, but I'm delighted to see you again."

"Oh, I'm so pleased to see you, Dad," Veronica said, stretching her arms to embrace him.

But when she tried, she felt nothing more than a rush of air coursing through her arms.

"Ah, I suppose I can't hug you. You're a... ghost? Have you been watching the goings-on in my life? In our family's life? Are you aware that Karina sold the family home?"

"Yes, I know," he replied. "That's one of the reasons I'm here. There are truths about our family, secrets only you should know. And I must relay them quickly before I disappear or anyone else knows about this place. Once revealed—and it will be—things will become far more complicated for you."

"This place? Do you mean the basement? Is this really our basement?"

"Indeed, it is."

"Then how on earth did our basement get here, in Mexico?"

"It's not so much a matter of 'where' as it is of 'when.' When you breached that wall, you entered a different time, returning to an era when I was alive, and we resided in the old Tucson house."

"Hold on, Dad. Are you suggesting you invented time travel? That's absurd!"

"No, no, I didn't invent it. I merely know how to locate the portals."

"What are you talking about, Dad? You're going to have to elaborate. This is uncharted territory for me."

"There's much I need to share with you. My illness struck so suddenly that I had no chance to inform you, or even caution you, about the family's complexities, about our bloodline."

"What's so special about our bloodline? What the heck does that have to do with time travel? Why withhold this information until now? And why didn't you tell me earlier?"

"Our lineage carries unique abilities, insights uncommon among humans. You've noticed your gift for communicating with animals, haven't you?"

"Yes."

"That's one aspect of our heritage. Another is the ability to locate time portals. I learned how to freeze a moment in time, keeping it intact. The reason this basement holds importance is that it safeguards our family's true treasure. Karina might have sold the house and profited from it, but she never acquired the truly valuable asset because it remains securely hidden down here. Your task is to locate it."

"What exactly am I searching for?"

"We'll get to that in due course. First, you have much more to learn before you'll be prepared to open that door. It's been enough information for your first day. Now, why don't you go get some more rest? Remember to keep that key safe. And don't tell anyone about this place."

"Ok. I've really missed you, Dad." Veronica had started up the stairs but turned back, and ran into her father's ghostly arms, which, this time, appeared to be physically there, almost knocking him over. Veronica felt his physical form with her hands.

"I'm so glad you're back," she said, as tears streamed hot down her cheeks.

"Me, too, Veronica. Me, too."

CHAPTER 4

She rolled over and realized it was morning, questioning whether the entire experience had been a dream. Yet, glancing at the beautiful dogs lounging on her bed, she felt a sense of certainty. Her unique connection with these animals couldn't be mere coincidence. Rudy, who was always known for getting his nose into the things he shouldn't, seemed to have something else in his mouth this morning. The dogs had followed her down into the basement, and it appeared that he had brought something back from there in his mouth. One request to "Drop it!" from Veronica and Rudy revealed a slightly wet red book with the word Diary emblazoned with half-inch gold letters on the front. Veronica grabbed the diary from Rudy and determined that it was her mother's diary she had found. She opened it to find the first diary entry having to do with meeting their grandmother, Gladys's mother-in-law, for the first time, and how much she wanted to impress her.

Sunday, Jan. 20, 1949

Today was the first day I was to meet Mrs. Litchfield, the person who is always on the society *page for good taste, modesty, and following the rules of Emily Post to the tee. I made sure to wear a hat to church, as is customary these days, and to not show my legs, and I dressed as conservatively as possible, while still following today's latest fashion trends to also keep the interest of my beau.*

Stephen picked me up and drove me to the church. That's where we met his parents. Mr. and Mrs. Litchfield were so polite and welcoming. Then we went back to their house for lunch. They made me feel so at home in their home. Everyone was so nice. I just love this family, almost as much as I love Stephen!

"Thank you, Rudy! That is an added pleasure I will get to have, getting to know how my parents got along with their in-laws! But now I want to go back for more revelations!"

Slipping into some shorts and tying her hair back, she decided to investigate the basement again. Had her father's apparition been real, or simply a figment of her imagination? Veronica was going to find out for sure.

Just as she was about to rediscover the hidden entrance in the outdoor utility closet, her nosy neighbor, Mrs. Hawkins, appeared. Although she adored Mrs. Hawkins—a retired librarian who had moved to the area with her late husband a decade ago—why did she have to show up now of all times?

"Hi, Mrs. Hawkins!"

"Oh, Roni, you know you can call me Lizzy. How's my handsome boy, Rudolph?"

Rudy seemed ambivalent about Mrs. Hawkins. While he generally approved of women, he seemed put off by the overpowering aroma of her Chanel No. 5 perfume. Nonetheless, its distinct scent made her approach unmistakable.

Riley, on the other hand, instantly loved Lizzy Hawkins and would try to follow her home if she didn't keep an eye on her.

"To what do I owe this unexpected pleasure of your presence?"

"I want to help you with cataloging your books."

"Oh, that's such a sweet offer, but I'm not sure I'm ready to do such a thing yet. I'm not that organized. I don't even have shelves yet."

As a former English teacher, she had amassed an extensive classroom library of both classic and contemporary fiction and nonfiction for most reading levels. After collecting these books for three decades, it was hard to part with her collection of illustrated poetry books that brought poetry alive for her teenage readers, or her collection of one-of-a-kind Holocaust books from survivors she had personally met after being a Holocaust educator for most of her career, or even her many resources on Shakespeare and his plays, a passion ignited by a transformative summer studying at Cambridge in England. These volumes had accompanied her every step of the way. She kept them, believing that they might one day be cherished by her children or dedicated to a cause equally close to her heart. maybe, just maybe, she could pass them on to her kids or find some other worthy cause.

Lizzy Hawkins had helped her find that cause. She met her at Al Capone's restaurant. Veronica was alone, eating lunch; so was Lizzy, and she saw her reading the latest Anne Hillerman novel. Veronica had just gone to the Tucson Festival of Books and the author spoke about her novel and continuing her dad, Tony Hillerman's characters, so she asked to eat lunch with her, and Lizzy and she had been book buddies ever since. She made her realize that it was her duty, her calling to share her books with others.

She started by putting flyers on the doors of everyone in the predominately American community of Las Olas. She began with the first five boxes she had opened and wrote down the titles and authors of the books. Then she provided her phone number and asked them to text her, leaving a list of the titles and authors of a maximum of two books, along with their name and address. She promised to deliver the books in three days. She thought it would be a fun way to get to know her neighbors. However, she soon realized that she was dealing with some old-school residents who didn't know how to text, so they inundated her voicemail, as well.

"My name is Ken Kilroy. I'd like to read Stephen King's *The Outsider*. I've always liked Stephen King movies, so I'm sure I'd like this book. I live at Lot 311, right off the beach, the one with the blue whale on the light post."

"Brigette Honeysuckle. Titles: *Huckleberry Finn*, Tom Clancy, and *Whirlig*. Ooh, that last one sounds different. I'll try it. Address: Lot 471 on Salida del Sol. I have a green door."

She was beginning to realize that she would need a map of Las Olas, and she might have to draw it out herself. But surely someone must have a map with all the lot numbers, and she did notice that there were street signs. In all the years of coming down here, they had always given directions like "Turn at the whale skeleton near the CEDO building" or "Make your first left," but they had never used street names and numbers in their directions. Mapping Las Olas with streets and numbers was going to be a new concept for her.

She knew exactly who she needed to meet to find such a map— the president of the HOA! Lizzy Hawkins seemed to be well-connected in the community, so she asked her if she knew him.

"Of course. I'll set up a meeting."

"I'd rather do this myself," she replied, not wanting to be rude but also keen on establishing her reputation separate from anyone else.

"That's fine. I'll give you his details."

"Thanks, Lizzy. I appreciate your understanding."

It was a good thing she handled it this way because this was how the meeting with the president of the HOA began.

"Before we begin, Ms. Frederickson, how did you get my number?" he inquired.

"Well, you are in charge of my HOA, are you not? So shouldn't

I be able to get a hold of you?"

"That is true," he conceded.

"Then there you have it," she said, settling the matter.

"The only reason I ask is because I have been constantly harassed, followed, and stalked by that Lizzy Hawkins woman. She seems like a sweet little librarian type, but she is nothing short of a nightmare, a pariah, relentlessly pursuing me!"

Veronica couldn't believe what HOA President Harry Hillsdale was saying about her nice friend Lizzy. Lizzy would never hurt a fly.

From that instant, she felt a growing disdain for this man. Hillsdale was miserable to be around and had no books in his house. He was not a well-read man, and that probably explained why he didn't like Lizzy. However, he did seem to have expensive tastes. As she surveyed his living room, the trappings of luxury were hard to miss: fine decanters of expensive whiskey, scotch, and wine, shelves filled with costly steins, and an array of weaponry. A stark contrast to the classics of great literature she and Lizzy would cherish.

"I am creating a library check-out system for the community and would like a map of Las Olas to help me deliver the books to people. Do you have one?" she asked.

"That has to get approved by the association," he replied.

"Why? They're my books. I'm loaning them to people through my phone plan."

"Oh. Well, it's a fine line... Especially if you are calling it Las Olas anything..."

"Well, I'll consider that. I kind of ran into some obstacles when I started my community newsletter."

"Well, we already had one." Then he kind of paused and looked up. "Oh, you're *that* girl. You sure like to stir the pot, don't you?"

"No, sir, I just like to let the community participate more in their newsletter by making it more personal and more literary."

"No one wants that,'" he stated, standing up as if the meeting was over.

She didn't move.

"Well, I've been getting a positive response."

He could see that she wasn't going to leave until she got what she came for, so he motioned for her to follow him into another room, and she obediently followed. As he walked, his demeanor seemed to relax, and she couldn't help but notice a white Pekingese dog trotting alongside him the whole way.

"This is Sam. Don't worry. He only takes small bites," he said with a hint of humor, and Sam barked in response and snapped his teeth, showing he knew what they were talking about. She laughed out loud, realizing that maybe this man wasn't as unpleasant as she had initially thought. Sam directed her to a picture of a wife, a boy, and Mr. Hillsdale.

The entire hallway they walked through was adorned with pictures of the three in all different settings, making it clear that they had been very active, but there were no pictures of the boy past age 10, and the wife never seemed to get gray hair, as Mr. Hillsdale had. When Veronica peeked into the kitchen, the lonely plate, glass, and bowl wallowed with the lonely song of a man who had lost it all.

She looked down at Sam, who had a tear in his eye. His dog knew something about him, and seemed to love him, and that spoke volumes. Was Sam trying to tell her something? Did she need to address something with this man? Perhaps the elephant in the room? It didn't always matter that it wasn't her business. "Mankind was her business," according to *A Christmas Carol*, that is, and Veronica always lived her life by the classics.

"Harry, I couldn't help but notice your beautiful family on the wall as we walked through your home. I know this is forward to ask, but did something happen to them?"

"Yes. How did you know that?"

"Well, I just kind of figured it out, and I—"

"Hey, wait a minute! Are you trying to do a human-interest story on me for your stupid newsletter? Because if you are, I say 'No thank you, Ma'am! And goodbye!'"

"No. I was just wondering if you wanted to talk about it. I get a sense about these things, and it just felt like you might want to talk about it."

They arrived in his spacious office, where he stopped at a filing cabinet, and hung his head. He started weeping and fell to his knees.

"That's my wife, Kathleen, and our son, John. Today was supposed to be our 35th anniversary. It happened on our 10th anniversary. We were going out to dinner to celebrate. A car accident. In one night, I lost my whole family, my whole future. Sam has been the only one I have had through it all. Tonight, if you hadn't called, I had already planned on ending it all."

"Well, you didn't see who was saving you all this time was Sam. He has been there for you the whole time? He was there tonight, nudging me to look at those pictures. He knew you were in trouble, Harry. He knew you needed to talk to someone. Dogs are incredible creatures. They know us and love us through it all."

Harry pulled out a filing cabinet drawer labeled "HOA Las Olas" and rummaged through the files until he found three papers and a booklet.

"I guess you'll still be needing these. They're available online, but here's a blank one. Here's a copy of the street map. And here's a copy of the Lot Map. I'm also giving you a copy of the HOA rules. Don't break them," he advised. As she had been talking with Harry, Veronica realized that he could no longer be left alone, especially after he admitted what he had been considering doing, so she texted her friends Dave and Irene Verducci and asked them if they could come over and stay with Harry, so he wouldn't be alone. She thought that it might be good for him to also get in contact with other family and friends that he felt close to, as he was going through a low time and needed some support. Veronica started looking into some possible intake centers where he might go for some support, as suicide was nothing to take lightly. Her training as a teacher had taught her that Always get people professional help and take people seriously when they say they are considering taking their lives. She had done so for her son Charlie when he had expressed those feelings after her divorce from his father, and Charlie said he was feeling like he wanted to kill himself. She took him in to talk to someone right away. They said Charlie hadn't planned it all out, so he was going to be okay. But she did everything she could after that for Charlie to make sure he would be okay. She moved to a new town, changed jobs, got him involved in band in high school and that is what saved him. Charlie found his niche in a band. He trimmed down with a marching band. Then he became really good-looking. He became social and got involved in the Student Council. He found people would accept him as different. He liked guys. So what?

Strangely enough, as she left, she found herself feeling that she had played an important role in Harry's life. And it was all because Harry's dog, Sam, had played a role in changing her perception. Dogs, she mused, had a way of knowing a person's worth of character, almost the same way they could sense the deepest underlying smells. This man was more likable than she had originally thought. But she never would have gotten to know him if it weren't for his dog, Sam, who cared enough about Harry to help save his life.

CHAPTER 5

With all that had been going on, Veronica hadn't had time to check up on her dad's ghost. She was beginning to feel almost normal again when the thought of him possibly still being downstairs in the secret basement crossed her mind. She had considered the idea that he might just be a figment of her imagination after all. Riley, her vibrant Corgi, her constant companion, today alerted her to the fact that he wasn't mere imagination. She had put Riley on her leash to take her out for her morning walk, but the dog was not heading toward their usual path but pulling her toward the secret recesses of the outside closet, the entrance to an underground world filled with emotional and supernatural webs.

Something was down there, or rather someone or Riley's watchdog tendencies would not have perked up. She quickly surveyed the surroundings. At 5:30 am, only a few construction workers were hammering away on a street nearby. She couldn't see them, so she was reasonably sure they couldn't see her. She locked the side door to the house, and together with the determined Riley, she disappeared into the closet and then descended the basement stairs. Riley was pulling at the leash with such determination that she knew this was happening. And there, at the bottom of the steps, stood her dad, a spectral soul, both familiar and otherworldly, giving off a comforting light.

"Sorry, I haven't come down in a few days. Truthfully, I hoped you were some figment of my imagination," she admitted, her voice quivering and heartbroken.

"Sorry to disappoint you, but you need me right now. Otherwise, I wouldn't be here," he replied.

"Oh, don't get me wrong. I feel very blessed that you chose to see me. It's just that I wish I could tell someone."

"Who would you tell? And who would believe you, anyway?"

"Well, I could show them. Then they'd believe."

"That would be disastrous for both of us. I would disappear, and you wouldn't know why I was here. At least let things play out and keep this secret until we figure out my purpose. And your purpose for needing to know your gifts. I will work with you to hone your skills. Then you won't need me anymore. How does that sound?" he suggested.

"That's fair. I've kept it a secret so far, so I guess I can keep doing that," she agreed.

"Good. Now, let's get to work on your skills."

"When did you first notice your special gift with animals?" he inquired.

"I knew there was something different about me when we had our first dog, Blackie. I would run behind Blackie, and he would protect me from anything or anyone like I was his little one. But it was more than just a man-dog relationship. There was something more. I spoke to him, and he listened," he recalled.

"You are correct. It is called Zoolingualism. Our family has this ability instilled in us," he explained.

"Perfect. Then you can teach me," she said eagerly.

"But each generation has had its special way of communicating with animals, and no one way has been completely figured out. It has been cataloged, "analog," and studied, and the bearer of such a gift reports his or her findings to the family head and then passes the findings on to the next generation," he informed her.

"I see. You never got to pass on your findings to me. Is that what you're saying?" she asked.

"Yes. You see, I, too, could talk to Blackie, but my gift was not quite as strong as yours. You also had a way with many other animals, which is why we thought you might become a veterinarian. But you chose to teach instead. We didn't want you to stand out too much, so we brought you back to live near us after you'd gone away to school in California."

"But why didn't you tell me then about my gifts?" she inquired.

"We weren't sure about them," he admitted.

"So, do I know how to develop my gifts with these animals?" she asked herself.

"Well, it's probably through practice, I'd say. Or is there a manual? I'd love that. Or a course I could take? Well, I've always learned best when I had to try to teach others, so maybe that's what I need to do: develop a manual myself."

She had figured it out. Nonverbal cues, their meanings, the swish of a tail this way or that, the raising of hair on a tail, the lifting of the edge of a mouth, a low growl, a loud growl, differing tones of growls – each had a meaning. What it was all about was communication. It wasn't magic; it was reading the cues and getting them right. Only those who were trained to read the cues could understand the animal. If that was considered magic, then so be it.

She sought a realm in which to practice her skills- and found Barb's Dog Rescue, a haven for the lost and abandoned, created by an American woman named Barbara who had a heart for the dogs that roamed the streets with no home. It was located just on the outskirts of town. There were at least a hundred dogs there, and they were always in need of volunteers. Veronica decided it was the perfect place to practice honing her nonverbal communication and verbal speech with the dogs. These dogs came from various backgrounds –some had been born there, while many had been abandoned by tourists or were lost.

One dog taught her a lot. His name was Troubadour, a Lhasa

Apso. His owner had lost him on a cruise ship passing by, and a local fisherman had found him floating. The fisherman performed CPR on him and brought him back to life before taking him to Barb's Dog Rescue. Troubadour had been at the shelter for two years, with no one wanting to adopt him due to his grayish hair and limp. He spent a lot of time with Veronica, hoping she would find him interesting enough to take him home. Veronica visited the shelter every day, listening, observing, and taking copious notes for her manual on animal communication, which she intended to use and pass down through the family, adding to the findings of her forefathers' notes.

Some of her findings were:

> Dogs use their incredible sense of smell to gather information about their environment, other animals, and humans. They detect pheromones, + chemical signals which tell them a lot about the emotions and intentions of others.

Troubadour was getting high hopes that Veronica would take him with her, but then he found out she had two dogs at home, named Riley and Rudy.

One day, Barb approached Veronica as she arrived at the shelter.

"I don't know if it's such a good idea that you are spending this much time with Troubadour. He is beginning to get too attached to you, and I'm afraid he is going to be heartbroken if you leave and don't take him home with you," Barbara expressed her concern.

"Oh, I see. I didn't realize how much of a bond I was forming with him. He is a terrific dog. I just didn't realize..."

"Yes, I'm afraid I can't allow you to meet with him anymore."

Veronica felt disappointed but understood the reasoning. "Do you think I could just say goodbye?" she asked.

Barbara hesitated for a moment and then conceded, "Well, okay."

She went into the meeting room where dogs and potential owners met, and Veronica gave him a heartfelt hug. Veronica just happened to drop her backpack amid that hug and out fell her mother's diary. Troubadour immediately fixated on it. He grabbed it and pawed at the pages to get to a particular one. He said in muffled tones to her, "Your Mom was in trouble."

Intrigued, she read the diary entry.

October 9, 1949

I am just so ashamed of what has happened to me. My life was going perfectly, but then this man had to come in and change it. I am just so worried about how my fiancé is going to take the news. He is so wonderful, but men do not like it when other men touch their women. I honestly thought I was being taken into a room for an interview. I am a good girl. I had no idea there were people like this in the world. Now I know that you need to travel in twos when you are in a big city like Washington, D.C. I did not even know what rape was or that it could happen to a good girl like me. He ripped my blouse, treated me like I was cheap, and then told me to get out! I screamed! I could not move. I was a beauty queen, I told him. I met Eleanor Roosevelt. He could not treat me like that. I was not a whore. I was not a prostitute. He had gotten me mixed up. He did not care. I do not know how this is going to change my life, but I know that it will. I am going to the hospital to get checked out.

As she read the diary entry, Veronica's face turned sheet-white and sweat ran down her brow. She could not believe this had happened to her mother. But she had to tend to the matter at hand. She communicated with Troubadour using her unique ability, saying,

"You and I can't meet anymore because we are getting too close. I will miss our time together. Do you want to live with me, or do you just want out of here?" she asked in dog language.

"I would like the freedom to choose where I live, but your house will be much better than here. I promise to be good," Troubadour replied.

As Veronica was listening to Troubadour's muffled dog sounds, she glimpsed a very worried Barbara behind the glass window, peeking in. The next thing she knew, Barbara and several of her helpers burst through the door. "Our dogs! Get out and don't come back!"

Knowing she had made a promise to Troubadour and that Troubadour had been helping her become more skilled at dog language and its interpretation, she begged, "Can I at least adopt a dog? Can I adopt Troubadour?'"

"You are the only one who has ever shown interest in him, so yes, I'll let you have Troubadour."

So, Fate, with its unpredictable trajectories made Troubadour not a mere fragment of Veronica's memory, but a part of her evolving story, as he, a once discarded soul, found sanctuary in the loving fold of her life. And, indeed, Veronica was beginning to see that the diary she had found was a key to the mystery behind her sister's strange behaviors.

When they arrived back home, now with a new member of the pack, Troubadour went to settle in with Rudy and Riley, while Veronica decided she needed to read more of her mother's diary.

Oct. 14, 1949

It's been a week since I last wrote. Stephen has been so understanding and loving about the whole thing. I got checked out at the hospital, and they sent me home, saying that I had been beaten up badly and that I had been raped. They asked me if I knew the man. I said I just met him for an interview. I had his name on a piece of paper that I handed to them. Rick Jordan. That name would forever haunt me. They said I needed to come back in a few weeks if I missed my period. Oh, my mercy! I might be pregnant with this man's baby. With my rapist's baby! That would be the worst! But Stephen reassured me that we are in this together and we will decide together what to do.

Nov. 15, 1949

It's been a month since I last wrote. I'm pregnant. But you know what! I'm not upset. Stephen said that we would have the baby grow up as ours. The father of the child wants nothing to do with it, so we're on our own. Maybe this was a test by God to see how strong my faith was. I don't know. I have been praying every night for the answer, and He has given me Stephen. He has been so understanding and loving through this whole ordeal when other men might have been upset. He supported me and realized that I did nothing to deserve this and wanted to move up our wedding date to better fit the timeline of our pregnancy.

Nov.16, 1949

We have decided on some baby names. If it's a girl, we're going to call her Karina, which is a variant of Carus, which in Latin means love; or David, which means beloved, if it's a boy. We want the baby to feel loved from the very beginning.

July 4, 1950

Dear Karina,

Happy Birthday! I just wanted to let you know that I only had fleeting thoughts at the beginning of not wanting you because of the rape. The rest of the time, I have wanted you every minute of this pregnancy, and I will love you every day of your life. You are my child, and I will always love you, no matter how you were conceived. You are a blessing that came to me, and I am so lucky that I get to have you in my life.

Veronica could not help but get emotional after reading these diary entries from her mother. She and her father had kept this secret from her all her life, but she didn't understand why. And she also did not understand why her father did not seem to trust Karina. There were lots of unanswered questions still, even if she knew this about her sister. Veronica was beginning to wonder why her dad would find Karina untrustworthy. Could she have had something to do with her father's early demise? She decided to order a copy of her father's autopsy report and medical records to check what the cause of death had been. She had this sent to her mailbox in Phoenix, so it would take a while to arrive.

CHAPTER 6

"Listen, Dad," she began, "I did get a chance to read Mom's diary. That must have been extremely hard for you and Mom to keep this a secret all those years. Did you ever tell Karina?"

"Well, that's the thing. We were going to, but she found the diary first, and read what you read, and it made her so furious that we did not tell her, that she started to turn on us."

"Whoa. When was that?"

"Right before my heart attack. But we had never treated her any different than the rest of you all during her childhood."

"Is there something else about Karina I should know?"

"I think it's great to have this ability to communicate with animals, but how is this going to help me get back at Karina and find the treasure? And Dad, why is it that you don't trust her so much, and want revenge? And what is this treasure anyway? More books?"

"I don't blame you for doubting me but keep it together. There is so much more awaiting you. Be patient. Do what I tell you, and you will go far. The animals will be there to help you when you need them. So put your trust in them, as well."

"I know. I realize that they are there for us, but I could use some magic spell right now!"

"If I tell you this, you can't use it without understanding it first. Got it?"

"What?" she asked, curious.

"You possess the ability to become invisible," he disclosed in a serious tone.

"Invisible?" Veronica questioned, with skepticism.

"Now that's something I'd like to try!" she exclaimed excitedly.

"Not yet! You have to understand the issues behind it..."

"Make me invisible!" she demanded impulsively, not realizing that those very words would make her invisible before her father could explain to her how to change back and the implications of this newfound ability.

The impetuousness of youth can sometimes lead to unexpected consequences when given great gifts, especially those involving significant powers. Such was the case with Veronica. She had been bestowed with an extraordinary gift, but she was squandering it and, sadly, losing precious time with her dearly loved father. The time she was invisible was taking away time her father was able to spend with her.

"This is so cool. How long can I stay invisible?" she asked.

"For up to 24 hours," he replied.

"And how do I stop being invisible?"

"You need to say, 'Make me visible,' but you need to know a few things first. You may not come back the same way. You will probably not have clothes on. And you have to keep track of the time. You only have 24 hours."

Veronica was beginning to understand that there were limits to this gift, so she said, 'Make me visible,' and instantly she returned to the basement, but only wearing her birthday suit, so to speak.

She quickly grabbed one of her mom's old afghans off a nearby box and wrapped it around herself to avoid embarrassment.

"I guess I was getting a little ahead of myself," she admitted with a chuckle.

Suddenly, Riley started barking, and this started Rudy howling, indicating someone was at the house.

"I would say so, but I guess we'll have to put this off until later. But come back soon. I don't know how long I can be here."

"Don't worry, Daddy. I will make you Priority Uno!"

Veronica needed to go back up to the "real world" of Mexico and life as she knew it. She looked at the time on the wall clock; it was still only 8 am. Who could it be at this hour? She had left her phone next to her bed, so she couldn't check the Ring app. Racing up the basement stairs, she felt light as a feather, because, as she had found out, she truly was "magical!"

Veronica quickly composed herself, utilizing the self-talk and breathing techniques she had learned from therapy and self-help webinars. She left the closet, pretending to choose a broom, all the while ready to wield it as a weapon if necessary. She turned around, brandishing the broom defensively, only to find Lizzy Hawkins approaching her from behind.

"Getting a clean start on the day?" Lizzy greeted her.

"Oh, Lizzy Hawkins, you startled me! You could've given me a heart attack, creeping up on me like that! Announce your presence next time!" Veronica scolded, her heart still racing from the surprise.

"Sorry. I was just getting an early start, myself," Lizzy apologized.

"It's okay. What are you up to?" Veronica inquired.

"I just wanted to help with the book deliveries today. Are you ready to get going?" Lizzy asked.

"Yes. Just give me a minute to jump in the shower," Veronica realized she had forgotten her promise to meet Lizzy early that day. "Go ahead and get yourself a cup of coffee, and I'll be ready in 15 minutes."

Veronica noticed Lizzy peering curiously into the supply closet, so she promptly shut and locked it to keep her from prying. Lizzy was taken aback by this dramatic action and commented, "Wow, I guess you must have all the treasures in the world in your broom closet."

"Well, you know what they say, 'One man's trash is another man's treasure!'" Veronica quipped, and they both burst out laughing.

"'Where your treasure is, your heart will be also'. You know where that comes from, right?" Lizzy asked.

"Yes, Jesus said it. Now, will you let me take a shower?"

Veronica deflected the conversation, wanting to avoid discussing her secret activities in the closet and basement. Her trust had been shattered by her sister, and her father had warned her not to trust anyone, not even her friends.

"Delivery for Jordan Mayhew," Veronica chanted as they approached the first door. "Here's your copy of *Fahrenheit 451* by Ray Bradbury."

And they were off, providing their service to the community.

CHAPTER 7

Her secret studies began. She would sneak down to the basement before her morning walks with Riley, ensuring that no one saw her. Under the cover of darkness, she would make her way through the iron door, across the outdoor garage, and into the storeroom closet. From there, she descended into the basement of her parents' past, where she would study magic with her ghostly father.

As Veronica cautiously walked further into the hallway passage lined with rows of bookshelves from her childhood, a sense of nervousness washed over her. She couldn't help but feel apprehensive, half-expecting a ghostly encounter or a potential attacker lurking in the depths of this underground space. The thought of being alone in this secluded basement, far from anyone's hearing, sent shivers down her spine. She scolded herself for entertaining such dark thoughts and tried to focus on the positive aspects of her discovery.

This secret underground "cave" was now her hidden sanctuary, a place nobody else knew about. It was a precious secret, entrusted to her by her father. But why had he chosen her over her siblings? What made her so special in his eyes? These questions swirled in her mind as she continued her exploration.

Veronica recalled her father's explanations about the caliche, the challenging layer of earth that made construction and gardening difficult in this part of the Southwest. It was a stubborn barrier that had to be drilled through to access the soil and water table below, making basements a rarity in the region. This knowledge shed some light on the uniqueness of her underground discovery.

Outside, the angry ocean waves pounded the shore, and the relentless wind whipped palm fronds into a frenzy. Although the hurricane was still some distance away, its impact on her small community was already palpable. Veronica likened it to an unwelcome guest, disrupting the peace and forcing everyone to hunker down. She realized that today was not the day to expect to see banana boats, shrimp boats, or the touristy pirate ship out on the Sea of Cortez. The entire community was at the mercy of the storm, grounded by its ferocity.

As the hurricane raged outside, Veronica realized that it was the perfect opportunity to visit the basement without any unexpected visitors dropping by. With the dogs securely in the laundry room and her phone connected to the Ring app for added security, she locked the front door and made her way into the closet under the stairs.

"Dad? Are you still here?"

"As long as I can be with you, I will..."

"Oh, gosh! You still startle me every time!"

"That's perfectly normal. Any news?"

Veronica shared some news with her ghostly father.

"Well, actually, Queen Elizabeth just died last night. I still remember our trip to England when I was six!"

Veronica's big 6-year-old green eyes open wide, as her mother leads her into the room. Her jaw dropped open, as she drew closer to examine the minute details of each bedroom in gilt gold, the horses in the stables below, the meat in the kitchen, the candelabra in the dining rooms, and the books in the massive library. Queen Mary's dollhouse in Windsor Castle was the castle in miniature, with every detail spot on, and this trip to England was the point in time where Veronica began her lifetime love of miniatures. Later that day, in the restroom or "loo" at the castle, was a moment she would never forget. She excused herself to go to the restroom, and her mother said she would wait for her. When she got into the loo, she was met with two elderly ladies, who greeted her thus, "You, boy, get out of here! You are not allowed in the ladies' room!"

Veronica ran out, crying. She hadn't liked the short haircut her mom had given her either, but her mother had said, "It's the latest thing!"

However, they happened upon a toy store that had all kinds of wonderful puppets and dress-up items. One item that Veronica found the most delightful was a Pippi Longstocking wig with long red braids.

"I would rather look crazy and like a girl than be mistaken for a boy again!" and she refused to take off her wig for the remainder of their European vacation, much to the dismay of her mother.

Veronica came back from her dream world.

"I remember that crazy trip and the wig I wouldn't take off!"

"Your mother hated that wig!"

"I know. That was part of the revenge I got. I was so mad at her when those ladies threw me out of the ladies' room!"

Her father gently reminded her, "Aren't you forgetting your summer at Cambridge?"

Cambridge University dining hall. No one would believe Veronica that it looked like the one at Hogwarts, with the long dining tables and long benches. The classes were held in the building around a courtyard. She rented a bicycle and remembered getting stuck at the roundabout, going around and around and around. And the Shakespeare class Veronica took allowed her to go to a special section that was under lock and key.

"Oh yes. You know, that is a love we always shared, Dad - libraries & books. I didn't know if I ever got to tell you that."

As Veronica spoke to her father, reminiscing about these times, she felt a mixture of nostalgia and regret for the time they had lost together. Her father responded, "I knew that from the time when you were a little girl, that you secretly stole my books to make a library in the garage. That's why I didn't get mad when I found out."

"Welcome to the Litchfield Library! You can only check out 2 books at a time!" Come over here and let me stamp them."

"Oh! my mercy! You even have a date stamp to say when the books are due!"

"Hi, Mom. Yes, I borrowed that from Daddy's office, too!"

"Hi Roni, can I borrow The Black Stallion?"

"Sure, Nancy, it's over on that shelf over there, next to the back door."

"Do I take the card out of the book and write my name on it?"

"Yes, and I stamp the paper in the book, so you know when it's due."

"OK, thanks. I will return it on Oct.5th."

"Well, I'm not sure how your father will feel about his books being loaned out to the entire neighborhood," Veronica's mother, Gladys laughed.

She sighed and continued, "You know Karina and Larissa always resented the fact that I never got in trouble."

Her father reassured her, "Well, you were not a bad kid at all. But I'd turned soft by the time you came along. It had been 13 years since I'd had Larissa, so I was a little lax with you."

Veronica reflected, "Maybe that's why I was so lax with my kids. They didn't even have a father figure. I just wish you had been around a lot longer. Maybe things would have gone differently."

Her father offered some wisdom, "You can't wish for the past to change. It cannot, so you have no idea what would have happened. Everything may have happened the same for all you know. But what you can do something about is your future. However, you can use your special power to make things better, or worse. I knew that if I told your sister about our power, she would use it for her selfish gain, just like she did when she got all the money from our house, and she didn't share it. But I knew you would be different because you have a kind heart, a giving heart, and you do things for the right reasons."

Veronica listened as her father explained why he had not shared the family's special gift with her siblings. She asked, "What about Larissa or Frederick? Why didn't you share this with them? They were in the right bloodline, weren't they?"

Her father replied, "Yes, but Frederick left the country and left the family for a long time, so he went astray. He wasn't reliable."

Veronica nodded, remembering Frederick's turbulent life. She added, "He did have a lot of different wives. I think it numbered 6 last count. He has had one in each country he's lived in Spain, Russia, France, Germany, Portugal, and now Nicaragua. He has had a kid with 3 of them."

Her father sighed, "Yes, and he depended on your mother and me to support every one of them. Did you know that? Don't get me wrong. We love our grandchildren - Robert, Michael, and Ronald. We just didn't expect to pay all their child support!"

Veronica was surprised to learn this and said, "No, I wasn't aware of that. I thought he was such a renowned artist that everyone was buying his art."

Her father explained, "No, in fact, I had to fund his first gallery, and several exhibitions, just to get his art seen!"

Veronica realized the strain this must have put on her parents and said, "I had no idea that you had been carrying him for so long. I'm sorry, Dad. No wonder Karina was so irritated with him. I just did not get why she was so irritated with me all the time. I was not trying to fail so badly with men. I just couldn't seem to find the right ones."

Her father reassured her, "Well, I don't think you were looking in the right pot, Veronica. I am glad you did explore some of the cultural avenues you did, though. I was proud of you for going to the Holocaust program in Poland and Israel. And you did continue to take classes to improve your craft and expand your knowledge. That expanded your teaching and showed me that you were all about lifelong learning. That's what a true daughter of mine would be interested in."

Veronica was curious about her other sister and asked, "But what about Larissa? She genuinely loves her daughters and has given you three beautiful grandsons. She has been independently wealthy because she married so well, so she has not had to rely on our family at all for handouts. She's even helped my kids a couple of times with paying for their braces."

Her father explained, "Larissa was another story. She and her family were self-sufficient money-wise. But she was so swept up with her own family's medical and psychological issues, and her issues, that she seemed too overwhelmed to take on something else. She also had a husband who could afford to take care of her. She was and is in a different income bracket than any of us because of her husband's six-figure government job. They have two million-dollar houses, one on each coast, and always could take care of themselves without any help from me."

"I'm guessing I have been too busy with raising my kids until the last few years, as well. Until they all finally moved out, or rather, I lost it all, retired because of my declining health, and I moved out."

"Your health is fine. I manufactured that heart attack for you."

"What do you mean?"

"I took over your body for a moment and gave you my pulse (which was none) and faked the heart attack!"

"I'm not at risk for a future heart attack?"

"You're perfectly healthy."

"So, why me? You did trust Karina more than me at one time."

"I trusted Karina with everything for so long, and thought I could trust her, but then she turned on me and your mother. You have had to work at a different income level than all the rest, serving as a public school teacher, and you never had the same privileges the others did, and you never seemed to be greedy about money, and fight about it, like the others did, so you have shown your true worth."

"I know that this is a tender subject, but I want to talk to you about your mother's suicide note". He handed her the note. She looked at it, remembering the sadness it brought the first time she read it: *Please forgive me for what I have done. I deserve to go to Hell for what I have done. Please burn my body so that some of me will get to heaven with the wind.*

"I never believed she wrote that note."

"She didn't really."

"How can you be so sure, Dad? It is in her handwriting. It just doesn't sound like her."

"Because one of our unique gifts is 'time capture' of the past. We can go back and take a piece of the past and kind of timestamp it to look at it for a while, like this basement, but we cannot change it. We can study it closely, however, for as long as we have it, so that we will have an idea of where things are in the future, even if people have renovated the building."

"So, you have gone back to the place and time when she wrote the note?"

"Yes. Karina was telling her what to write."

"But why was she agreeing to write it?"

"Well, for one, your mom had Alzheimer's and believed everything Karina was telling her. And two, because she was holding a gun to her head, and told her she was going to make it look like a suicide."

"So, Karina killed Mom? Her mom? Just because she did not tell her she had a different father? That is messed up! That is simply wrong, Dad!"

"I agree. The Universe agrees. That is why I am here. To set things right."

"What we never heard was your mom asking Karina to promise to tell you that she loved you. She also had your mom rewrite the will at the lawyer's office a month before she died, leaving everything in her charge, but promising verbally that she would make sure everyone would get their fair share. She was never planning to include you in anything."

"Yeah. That is when Karina said Mom had left her everything - the house, all her money, and she was selling the house. Of course, I only received the $100,000 that we used to buy our house. That was it. She cleared almost a million. And then she decided to settle down with one of her gambling partners. And our beautiful home, my cherished childhood home, was gone. But money was more important to her. At least she kept Mom's paintings. She cared about her at least that much."

"She just kept them because she thought they were worth something. Don't kid yourself. Anyway, you don't have to worry. You are going to avenge our family's name by reclaiming the treasure that she lost in selling the house."

"So, the treasure is in the house? In Tucson? And I have to break in? Oh my. I guess I am going to need a lot more skills! I didn't think I was going to be participating in criminal activity."

CHAPTER 8

As a new day dawned in Puerto Bella, Veronica awoke to a new reality. She was being called to do more with her life than she had ever dreamed. Her father's final mention of "treasure" had kindled an electrifying spark within her and she sprung from her bed, her feet carrying her quickly and quietly down into the basement, a place steeped in history and forgotten by time. Having encountered a ghost and traveled the corridors of time right in her own home, the possibility of unearthing hidden riches seemed not just likely, but almost certain. Her heart pounded with anticipation as she descended into the depths once more, where secrets and fortune surely awaited.

At the first sight of her father's ghost, she ran up to him and blurted out, "Can you teach me how to go back in time to do that 'time capture' thing? Does it only work on your own past experiences, or can you do it with others' pasts, as well?"

"Well, hello, nice to see you would have been a nice start, but I guess you've been thinking a lot about this."

"I'm sorry, Dad. I guess I got a little overanxious when you said the word 'treasure!' I have to admit."

"Anyone would. I'm glad you're eager to learn. So let's get to work. Yes. Anyone's past is accessible," he explained, "but you must understand the weight of knowing certain things. It can still change a person's path going forward. Some things are not supposed to be known. There are some things that morally should not be known. So just remember to be careful about what things you choose to reveal to people."

"Alright. I will be."

Under the soft glow of the basement's lone bulb, Veronica's father, Stephen Litchfield, imparted the method of transforming a regular closet into a gateway to various times and places. By inscribing the date, time, and circumstances in a peculiar, coded language he had taught her, and employing deep concentration, she could extract that specific moment out of the meridian of time, especially on the night of a full moon. A crucial component was securing the door with a specialized key, which had to be concealed where only a particular individual might find it.

The quest for such keys led Veronica through antique stores until she encountered a locksmith, Hernando Mantequillo, in the town. His assurance was comforting yet curious.

"Señora, there's no need to scour old stores for these keys. I have old doors, locks, and keys that can serve your purpose. Let me show you in the back."

A hesitant pause lingered as Veronica contemplated trusting a man named 'butter' in Spanish—could he be 'slippery'? Nonetheless, curiosity guided her forward.

"Okay. Lead the way."

Indeed, he did have an assortment of keys and locks, an almost museum-like collection at the back of his shop, displaying a rich history of door accessories. It was the world's oldest lineup of door locks, door handles, doorknobs, door knockers, door frames, doors, skeleton keys, and old-time keys that looked like they were from times past. They were made from different alloys of metal - copper, brass, gold, steel, aluminum, tin, and silver. Some were rusted, while others were shiny and bright, and a few were cobwebbed. A wide variety filled the small shop to the brink. From then on, Hernando became her go-to for locks and keys.

It was only later on that he started to ask questions.

"Why don't you use modern locks and keys? They are much cheaper and easier to use."

Veronica was prepared with her answer: "I suppose I'm just old-fashioned."

That answer stopped the questions for the time being.

Some of her new adventures were beginning to make her act a little more on edge. She was becoming more suspicious of everyone around her, thinking that everyone was out to get her or find out about her family. She was becoming more miserly and mean.

One day, she caught herself in the mirror on the way out the door. Had she become so negative and rude? Who was this person scowling at her? She resolved to figure out a way to regain the positive disposition she had once possessed. The moon held the key.

She decided to focus on the one thing she knew was the most important. That was what she was supposed to do. "Chase two rabbits. Catch neither." was the Chinese proverb her father used to tell her. She tried to recall the many times she had repeated that quote in her college dorm room as she attempted to study instead of going out socializing with her sorority sisters!

One night, unexpectedly, Veronica was sitting on her porch with her dogs at her side when she received a text message from her middle son, Harry: "Are you all right, Mom? Aren't you scared in that big house, all alone at night? Someone could just come in and knife you to death, and we would not know. And you'd be lying there for weeks before we got the call if we ever would."

"Thanks for the vote of confidence, son," she texted back.

"Well, it's not that I don't trust you; it's the other guy. The one that might take advantage of you," Harry replied.

"Don't you think I am smart enough to recognize when people are scamming me?"

"Well, yes and no. We've just heard too many stories of our friends whose parents did not see it coming. So let us know who you meet. Let us check them out. Okay?" Harry replied with real concern in his voice.

Of the three boys, Harry always seemed to call and wonder how she was doing. He seemed to care what happened to her.

"Oh, I know how to read people," was her final reply.

When she went to bed that night, she felt more alone than usual. The house carried a louder echo. She went around, locking all the doors and making sure all the windows were latched. She pulled her covers up tighter around her head and even let the dogs sleep in the room.

❧

THE NEXT MORNING, SHE WENT DOWN EARLY TO THE BASEMENT and did her training with her father's ghost, but even her father noticed there was something different about her.

"What is going on with you today? You are in a very different mood."

"Harry said something last night and made me realize how lonely I am."

"Oh, come on. You have got the dogs, and I am here!" Even though her father seemed to laugh sarcastically, knowing that that was not what she meant.

""Do you know that I have not kissed a man for nearly 10 years!"

"And why is that?"

"Because every time I tried to date someone, my boys would scare them away. They would not let me date anyone and controlled my life after my last divorce, so I could not get close to anyone. It was ridiculously hard on me. But I think they did it to protect me."

"Well, you're wrong there. They did it to protect your money. They wanted to make sure their inheritance was not going to someone else. Unfortunately, money is more powerful than blood.

I had to learn this the hard way with your sister. You will have to learn this the hard way with your sons."

"I can't believe that they just want my money."

"In the end, that's what they all fight about. That is why you must divide things yourself, so there is no fight. You decide."

"You may be right, but Harry seems to care about me. And he was still right about one thing - I am lonely. I felt so lonely and afraid. I knew you were down here, and that gave me some comfort. I have my dogs, but there's something about having another human with you that puts your heart at ease."

"I know what you mean. Every time we had to move to a new Army base - New Jersey, Arizona, Peru, Germany, France, Florida, Africa - we didn't always know the language or customs, so we were like fish out of water. Your mother made it so much easier for me. She was my teammate. She'd say, 'We're in this together,' and we'd do our best to learn what we needed to get groceries and do basic things while we were there. It is easier working as a team than as an individual player sometimes."

"I mean, there are still good things about being single, though. You don't have to fight about what show to watch, which place to go, which car to buy, which dog to get, where to go for dinner, etc., but the big decisions sometimes help to have another person's input, like whether to take a certain job, invest in something, or trust someone with something important. You've probably found that out the hard way."

"I didn't realize mom was so with it."

"She has always been the one who has held our family together through thick and thin. Your mom was always the one with the toughest skin. Don't let her femininity fool you. She may have been a beauty queen and loved jewelry and fashion, but she was determined to get our family through the toughest of times and do so with panache. She wanted all of her children to be able to go to college."

"Mom was great, Dad. But I think you're missing my point

about me. What do you think about me going on online dating again?"

"Do you think it's wise to meet people here in Mexico?"

"I don't know if I'll meet them here. They might be in Phoenix. Or Arizona. Close by. The point is I will have to communicate with them a while before I will even meet them."

"Well, one word of warning. Don't ever tell them about this place or me, or your magic. Other people just won't understand. It took a very long time for me to tell your mother."

"So she knew? Did she have any magical abilities?"

"No. It was on my side - the Shipley side of the family. And yes, I had to tell her because I knew our children could have magical abilities, and I'd have to prepare her for that possibility."

"How did she take it when you told her?"

"I didn't have to tell her. She covered for me one time when I came back from being invisible at the wrong time, wrong place—she kind of pushed me out of sight, so no one could see me naked. She said she knew there was something different about me, and she loved me anyway. That's when I knew I had found the right woman."

"Well, then eventually I might have to tell a person, or they might find out."

"Perhaps, but it will only be if you know them for a long time, and completely trust them."

"Okay, I understand."

CHAPTER 9

Veronica put her profile on the dating site. She wasn't the thinnest woman in the world, weighing 240 pounds, but she had a fun personality. She got a couple of hits. Talked to a few people for a while. Then she talked to one guy for a week and decided to meet him.

As she parked at the Mi Amigo Ricardo Restaurant, she noticed a man standing near the door. It was Robert. He matched his profile photo to a tee. Suddenly, it was as if the lights in the sky were cued to make the perfect amber sunset glow at dusk, the mariachi music playing Mexican love songs lightly in the background, and, as if out of a movie, Robert smiled and walked over to her car, opening the door for her.

"Hello, Veronica. I'm Robert Fierro," he said, offering her his hand to assist her in getting out of the car.

"Hello," was all that Veronica could utter, being thrown off by this gentlemanly deed.

"Shall we go inside?" He offered her his arm, and she gladly grabbed hold.

"Good evening. May I help you?" the host asked.

"Two for dinner, somewhere quiet where we can talk, please?" Robert requested.

"Certainly, sir. Right this way."

After they were seated, Robert shook his head, saying, "You are so much prettier in person. I am just blown away."

Veronica was turning noticeably red. She could feel her cheeks getting hot and put her hand to her face to cover her embarrassment.

"You just say what you're thinking, huh?"

"I'm a straight shooter. I don't pull any punches. I did marry once, I've been divorced for 10 years, and I don't plan to marry again."

"I see. Well, I am kind of the marrying type. I hope that doesn't scare you off."

"I don't scare easily."

With that, Veronica knew that Robert might have potential. Every night that week, Robert called. It appeared they were becoming a couple.

Of course, when Veronica called her sons on speakerphone, they had another thing to say about it.

Charlie, the youngest, spoke up first, "You know, Mom, I don't think you should be dating. Aren't you too old to date?"

"And why, pray tell, not?"

"I agree with Charlie, Mom. Someone might be trying to just get your money," Joseph said.

"And what about you, Harry, you're the middle son. What do you have to say?"

"I think Mom is old enough to make her own decisions, but we still want to approve the guy, so you don't make a bad decision."

"Well, I can make my own dating decisions. I'm not too old. I've already met someone."

And, with that, Veronica hung up the phone.

Later that night, she received a text message from Charlie, her youngest, which said, *You never did seem to care about us, Mom. You only care about yourself, and sex. I wish you were dead.*

Robert had come over for dinner and was walking in from

placing the steaks he had brought on the grill outside. He noticed Veronica was noticeably upset, her eyes welling up with tears.

"What is it?"

"Oh, it's just my silly reaction."

"To what?"

"My sons don't like me dating."

"What? That's ridiculous. You're a grown woman, not a child!"

"Let me read what they said."

"No, it's not very nice."

"Well, then that's not good at all. Let me see."

Robert read aloud, "'You never did seem to care about us, Mom. You only care about yourself, and sex. I wish you were dead'."

"That is just disrespectful and wrong to say to one's mother! And how old is Charlie?"

"He's 25."

"He has some issues."

"He has never really had a father figure he could count on. I've been married three times, all to men who left me financially in ruins and for other women. There's been a pattern of men I couldn't count on."

"Well, I'm good at finances. I am a banker. I have worked at several banks, and done real estate, and I can help you with your financial troubles. But your kids have no right to talk to you like that. You are their mother! If I spoke to my mother like that, she would slap me across the face! I was not the perfect kid, but I always treated my mom with respect. I always tried to help her with the dishes or to clean up the yard."

"Well, my boys have not had the best role models for that, but I have tried my best. At least they helped to move me here. That was something. But I don't know how much more support I will get from them. My youngest is not going to support our relationship."

CHAPTER 10

Veronica continued to try to make her Mexico house a home by putting up all her beautiful paintings that her mother had painted, along with her four Van Gogh paintings. In fact, Robert came up with the idea to make her kitchen a "Van Gogh Kitchen" by putting one painting on each of the four walls of the room. The vivid blues and yellows of "Starry Night," "The Café," "The Bedroom," and "The Church" really brought the little kitchen alive, their grandeur overlooking the space.

"I adore it, Robert! It resembles a gallery! Now we should paint the kitchen the Van Gogh blue!"

Veronica looked over at the wall where she had hung the almost life-sized photo of her father and painting of her mother and, suddenly, remembered her father's ghost—in the basement, silently waiting for her all this time. The guilt started to gnaw at her heart. How long had it been since she had been down there? Since she met Robert? Had it been a month already? She had let him get in the way of her relationship with her ghostly father. Or had she wanted to forget? Her mind was playing tricks on her.

She could have lost him. He could have disappeared by now. All because of a guy. Just like her son warned. Was he right? All she cared about was... sex? That couldn't be true. She had to stop thinking that way and get down to the basement. And she had to do it undetected by Robert. Now she had an added problem. He was now living with her. Yes, she had let him move in with her. And she hadn't thought over one big problem- the ghostly one.

The following morning, Veronica, ever the early riser, slipped out the door, allowing only a singular ray of sunlight to creep through a gap in the room-darkening curtain. She snuck into the outside storage closet, where she turned the key to the door to the secret basement that she hoped was still there. Down the steps, she ran quickly but quietly, while the door magically muted the outside noises above.

When she got down the stairs this time, the musty basement smell of cedar, old newsprint, and wet books snuffled her senses. She saw the books, comics, record albums, law books, Reader's Digest series, and joke books that her father had cluttered the walls with from toe to ceiling. Her childhood basement of books came back alive, as did the father she once knew. His visage warbled in front of her this time silently, and she had to do all the talking. Somehow the spirit world had taken away his speaking abilities, and their only means of communication was his gesturing. The month away had divorced him of his speaking abilities. She should not have stayed away so long. Now she had lost the valuable wisdom his words could have imparted to her, and she regretted the pull that loneliness had had on her heart. She had sacrificed one love for another. Family love for romantic love.

"I am sorry I have stayed away so long. I know that I have missed out on some of your wise words, Dad."

The ghostly visage came over and picked up her head now hung in remorse and handed her a book.

"Okay, Dad, I understand. Do you want me to study this book? You are pointing to the title that says Litchfield Family History? So that is what I need to know?"

Her father's ghost nodded in agreement and settled in his chair as she began reading.

The unfolding information seemingly contained the knowledge her father wished her to grasp:

The Litchfield family fortune had always been intricately tied to gold, a bounty so easily procured that it became a curse, drawing people to marry into the family for access to these abilities. To protect their secret and their wealth, they concealed their abilities, altered their family name, and hid the gold, ensuring only blood relatives were privy to this secret and their capabilities. Stephen Litchfield Sr., Jr., and now III, her father, had incidentally acquired a shipment of what became known as the Lost Confederate Gold, a treasure whose destiny and handling still hung in the balance.

"So, this is what you wanted me to know?"

Her father's ghost nodded in agreement. Then he made her come with him, and she followed. He took her to a wall under the stairs and pointed to a tape measure on the floor. She picked it up. He pointed to a small wooden door right under the stairs. She started to measure it, but he shook his finger no. He pointed to the space above and the space to the wall.

She measured those and wrote those measurements down on her phone. Then he motioned for her to open the door. She looked at the clock and realized that the 'real world' would be rising soon, and Robert would be looking for her. She knew she had to tell her father about him.

"Father, I've met someone. His name is Robert, and he's the reason for my absence. He's a good man, and I trust him. He's moved in upstairs, and I need to get back before he starts looking for me. I haven't told him about you yet," she explained.

For the first time, her father got up enough energy to write a response: "You can never tell him, Veronica. He can't be trusted."

"I believe I can trust him."

In his last surge of energy, he wrote: "I'm saving your life, believe me."

"Okay, Daddy, I believe you."

Just as Veronica was coming out of the storage closet, with a broom in hand, Robert appeared.

"Veronica, why are you up so early? You should not be working this early. Why don't you come upstairs, and I'll make you a cup of coffee and breakfast?"

"That sounds heavenly. Thank you," she responded, thankful that Robert appeared unaware of her alternate world - one of enchantment, ghosts, and un-shareable secrets. Even if she attempted an explanation, would he perceive her as delusional?

"Why jeopardize what we have?" she pondered silently. "He truly is good for me. He appears to care deeply; he's even uttered those three magic words. He listens to my stories and shares tales of his life, yet we're so different. To an outsider, we might not appear to be a match, but he chose to love me, and I love him. We compensate for each other's weaknesses. His critical nature and inability to see the bigger picture, his impatience even when there's no need, sometimes make it tough. I must exercise patience with his impatience."

"Hello, lover. What makes you so cheerful today?"

""I guess I just like having a man like you around, one who doesn't judge me for my looks and who takes me for who I am.""

"But of course. You're terrific. You're beautiful, fun to be around, you have a great personality, you're great in bed, you're smart, the whole package. I feel like I won."

"See, why can't other guys say nice things like that? I guess you're my one in a million!"

"We are going to have Thanksgiving at your mom's house and we're inviting everyone? Right?"

"Yes, I think we should just let the cat out of the bag and let them all know that we are a couple!" And, with that, he leaned over and gave her a strong embrace.

After catching her breath, she said, "Okay, that sounds like a plan to me."

Robert was a distraction. She was very enamored with his sultry, smooth ways. He also had encouraged her to get her weight loss surgery after all, since it had been very successful for him in shedding the pounds, and she had already shed 60 pounds in the first few months following the surgery. He had helped her to get healthier, feel better about herself, and get her finances in order. He was just an all-around great guy.

However, Veronica was so caught up in Robert that she suddenly realized one day that, before she went anywhere, she would need to learn a lot more from her father about what was in that room under the stairs, or she was not going to have enough information to help protect her family fortune from the likes of her sister.

Veronica was very worried that the information in the house could get into the wrong hands if she couldn't somehow get into it in real-time and somehow restore whatever needed to be extracted to its rightful owners- her family. She needed to get back to her father's ghost and start asking some direct questions. Maybe with his ability to write, she could get him to reveal more about the treasure and how she could get ahold of it. However, she still had to work around Robert. He was getting in the way.

Veronica thought that maybe there was some way she could get him out of the house for a while so that she could work with her father's ghost to make this happen. That might be the answer. She knew Robert needed to have some time with his daughters who were back in Pennsylvania. Maybe he needed to plan a trip to go back there, without her at first. There was a graduation coming up. Maybe she could act very unselfish, and not go to the graduation ceremony, and make the ceremony about his daughter and not about his new girlfriend.

That way, it looked like Veronica was playing the good girlfriend. And she could resolve some things with her father's ghost at the same time, while Robert was away, and he would be able to spend some bonding time with his daughters, which would be good for him, which would be a win-win for both sides. And she could get the house locked up for a bit, for when she was traveling, and then they could all meet at his mom's house for Thanksgiving, and Veronica could be the super cool unselfish girlfriend, and everyone would love her.

"Oh yes, baby, I will miss you terribly while you are gone, and I will call you every night, and we can go to sleep on the phone together."

"Oh, I would like that very much. Almost like reaching out and touching you. But you've got to understand that I am a very jealous kind of person. I don't like you talking to other guys."

"I'm not talking to any other guys. You're my guy. I'm a one-guy gal."

"That's good. I'm glad to hear that."

Off Robert drove in his silver Pilot. He was one of those neutral-is-better kinds of guys, who was very different from Veronica, whose car choices had always veered toward bright red or flashy blue. She had kind of a showy personality. Whereas Robert liked to live under the radar. He had told her stories about himself that would probably have made her mom cringe.

Was it true that she liked him because he was a 'bad boy?' The first night they had slept together, he had offered her harder drugs, to which she said her line,

"I'm high on life; I don't need that stuff."

"I'm planning to get off this, just so you know."

"Well, I was a teacher. I just can't bring myself to do any of that stuff. Maybe pot. But even that is illegal in Mexico, and I don't plan on spending any time in a Mexican jail! I hope you don't either."

CHAPTER 11

Veronica sometimes questioned why she was with this man who was so different from her. Soon after they met, Robert went off hard drugs, pot, cigarettes, and alcohol, all because he was around her. He had been living with his mother in Phoenix, trying to cope with her beginning dementia and grief over her husband's death.

She was going to meet the mom for the first time at Thanksgiving and was nervous about the encounter. She had met his daughters on the phone, and they were lovely.

"Hi Roni, this is Bella."

"Hey Bella, so nice to finally meet you."

"My dad sounds so happy, and I'm so glad you have helped him get off some of that stuff he was on."

"Well, Bella, that was all his doing, not mine."

"I know, but you were a great influence, so thank you."

"Your sister, Alex, is graduating, I understand. I just wanted to let you know the reason why I am not coming is not because I don't want to; I do, but because your dad and I think the spotlight should be on her; not your dad's new girlfriend. We don't want to take anything away from her special day."

"You are so cool, Roni! My dad is really lucky to find someone like you."

"Well, I feel like we're both lucky! Did you know that your sister Alex and my son, Charlie, have the same birthday? The same day, and year? There has to be some reason that God brought us together."

"Oh Roni, you are the treasure his heart has been seeking."

Veronica knew that Isabella genuinely meant what she had said, but why did the lovely sentiment not "feel" good? It was the word "treasure" that struck an off chord in her and sent a chill through her. She decided to not let it worry her for today, but she still knew that her father had told her she had special abilities in recognizing things, and this was not something she should forget, so she took out her diary and wrote down the incident.

Veronica had also been able to talk multiple times with Alex, Robert's younger daughter, who was studying to be a science teacher. She was very intelligent and read lots of books, and they connected on an intellectual level because of their love of books.

"Alex, you're a good poet. Maybe move a couple of lines around. That's it. You know what you're doing. I think you could enter these into a contest and easily win. Just go for it. It just kind of depends upon what voices they're looking for sometimes."

"Thanks, Roni, that works. Yeah, I know that not everyone accepts me as a poet because I want to teach science, but I also love literature and learning."

"Hey, you can love a lot of things. That's called being well-rounded. Don't just settle for being one thing, in one area. My dad was a 'Renaissance Man.' He was in the Army, in the Medical Corps, but he read so many books about all topics; his dad was a lawyer, so he studied law books, he studied languages, learned about computers before everyone else, was interested in other cultures, brought strangers home to dinner so we would learn about other interesting parts of the world. He learned about everything, and he kept learning till the day he died. And everyone respected him for that. I want to be like him. Everyone should be like him. You need to be you and keep learning to become an even better you, wherever that takes you."

"I'm so glad my dad met you, Roni. I need to have someone encourage me like this."

"No problem. Your dad and I are always here for you, Alex. Call any time."

When Robert left for his daughter Alex's graduation, it was a good time for Veronica to talk to her father's ghost and try to put together this picture of Robert she had been developing in her diary. She needed to talk to her father and figure out what she needed to still learn about the treasure, whether she should trust Robert with any of her secret life, what her future was going to look like going forward if she stayed with Robert, or if she should even stay with Robert. So, early the next morning, she woke and quietly went to the outside closet door. She turned the key and rushed down the steps, and he was there.

"Thank God. I was afraid you wouldn't even be here."

Her father's ghost opened wide his arms and clasped her, the treasured pearl of the oyster. Veronica felt like she was home again, after a long voyage. She shared her concerns about Robert with her father.

"If I feel a chill down my spine when his daughter says the word 'treasure' about Robert, what does that mean?"

Her father pointed to the family history book.

"Yes, I read it. Is there something in there about getting a chill down my spine?"

Her father nodded in agreement, and she began searching the book for answers. Then she came to the page, which read:

The individual exhibits a heightened sensitivity to unverbalized, yet potentially known, information possessed by another party. This sensitivity is uniquely characterized by the physical sensations triggered by the verbal expressions of the communicating party. This suggests an intrinsic, perhaps psychophysiological, connection between the recognition of concealed or unspoken knowledge and the senses.

"So I can feel when someone is lying to me? Or giving me hints about a person? Even if they don't mean to?"

The ghostly figure nodded.

"Does this mean Robert is not to be trusted?"

Again, he nodded.

"If I just break it off, he still could do something. Maybe I need to include him in the plan. But I need to outsmart him. What do you think? Can you help me?"

Her father's ghost nodded, but quickened to the dusty mirror and outlined the word 'Dangerous!'

No sooner had the word appeared, than it faded, but the chill of fear it gave her remained. Was Robert an enemy? How could someone be so kind, even sleep with her, and say he loved her? And even have his children believe it? Or were they in on it, too? Was this just too good to be true? Was she just too gullible? Too trusting? Too desperate? Not seeing what was there? Was her heart getting in the way of her head? Was she blinded by love? If only she could replay some of her dates with him, then she would know. That wasn't humanly possible... But she wasn't quite human, was she? She was a little different than normal humans. Maybe there was a way.

Veronica's plan to use the voice-activated recorder to uncover the truth about Robert seemed like a reasonable approach to her. She knew that her unique abilities allowed her to manipulate time in certain ways, and this could potentially provide her with the answers she needed.

She went to Robert's apartment, which felt strangely foreign to her since they hadn't spent much time there. She carefully searched for the right moment, the right time, to place the recorder where it would capture the truth about their relationship. She thought back to when they first met and decided that would be the ideal moment to focus on.

With the recorder hidden in place, she activated its voice-activated recording function and then left the apartment. She needed to give it time to capture whatever conversations or interactions might occur in the past. As she returned to her place, she couldn't shake the feeling of unease and uncertainty that had taken root in her mind.

The coming days would be filled with anticipation as she waited for the recorder to accumulate enough information. Once she had gathered the recordings, she would finally be able to listen and determine whether her instincts were correct or if her feelings for Robert were genuine and trustworthy.

She went back onto the dating site she had been using and got the date she had first spoken to Robert. She revisited her initial conversations through email as/ well. He was very forward right away, and she was quite surprised at how quickly he had expressed his love for her when she reviewed their text messages.

They had both laughed at how he had made such a bold move after only two weeks of knowing each other, saying, "When you're older, you know these things."

Now, she was beginning to realize that things had moved a little faster than she would have typically preferred.

Veronica decided to act. She was determined to find out the truth about Robert. She had a unique opportunity to revisit the past and learn what kind of man he was, at least in part, by listening in on his conversations from the beginning. She went over to his apartment and asked her dad to guide her through the steps of going back in time.

"Okay, Dad, so this is how it works, right? I've written down the date and time from a month before we met," she said, holding up the paper.

"I've also installed one of the special locks and keys that I bought from my locksmith friend on the closet door," she added with a giggle, demonstrating the key in the lock.

"Now, I will focus all my energy on that specific date and time, encoding the door lock with the special language you taught me," she explained.

Veronica recited the incantation:

Lock of old, key of gold;

> *Let us know the story told,*
> *When the truth before we hold.*
> *Grant us time upon this date*
> *To open up this hourly gate.*
> *If our intention should be ill,*
> *May our mortal blood be spilled.*
> *That our intention be just,*
> *To the Door of Time, we entrust.*

She continued explaining her plan, "When I am in that time, I can't be seen, so I will discreetly place the voice-activated audio recorder under the metal table or behind the door, quickly ensuring no one sees me. Then, I'll exit and lock the door again, repeating the words you taught me so that only I can open the door at that time to find out who Robert is."

With that, she chanted the words:

> *Key of gold, turn Lock of old;*
> *Let the truth finally be told.*
> *You know my intention to be just;*
> *Door of Time, only to me entrust.*

Her father's expression appeared pleased as he clasped his hands together, shaking them in admiration. Veronica could barely discern a smile on his face, as his figure seemed to be growing fainter.

Veronica's emotions overwhelmed her as she cried out, "Are you leaving me? You can't, Father! I still need your help. I don't know what the treasure is, how to get to it, how to carry it, or the answers to so many questions. Why are you leaving me?"

Tears streaming down her face, she collapsed onto the floor in Robert's apartment on the other side of Puerto Bella, Mexico. Her crying must have been quite loud because there was a knock at the door. It was the neighbor.

"Are you okay in there?" the concerned neighbor inquired.

Veronica hastily wiped away her tears and opened the door, trying to regain her composure.

"Oh, hi. I'm Veronica, Robert's girlfriend," she replied shakily. "I was just upset since he left, I guess."

"You're his girlfriend?" the neighbor asked, eyeing her up and down. "You don't look like a snotty rich girl to me."

Veronica was taken aback.

"Well, thanks, I guess. Is that the way he described me? And who are you? His best friend I've never heard of?"

"I'm his neighbor, John Sipes," he introduced himself, extending his hand for a handshake, which she reciprocated.

"We used to talk about his conquests with girls. Until he started dating you, that is," John explained.

"Really?" Veronica responded, surprised by this revelation.

"Yes, he's been with a lot of low-life girls. He finally got with you. It was the best thing that ever happened to him. I guess, since I knew you were rich, I thought you'd be stuck-up, too."

"Well, I'm not that rich, either. More middle class. But what do you mean, you knew I was rich?" Veronica inquired, puzzled by John's comment.

"That's all Robert could talk about after he met you, how loaded you were, how he'd hit the jackpot. I mean, he liked you, too, but he liked your money!" John explained.

Veronica absorbed this information with a mix of emotions.

"Hmm, well, thanks for the insight," she said, deciding to put an end to the conversation by shutting the door. She was tired of hearing about it and wanted to hear it from Robert's mouth.

Veronica was still grappling with the recent disappearance of her father's ghost, but she knew she had to unravel the mysteries recorded on that tape from the past. She inserted the key into the lock while reciting the incantation:

> *Lock of old, key of gold;*
> *Let me know the story told,*
> *When the truth before I hold.*

Grant me time upon this date
To open this hourly gate.
If my intention should be ill,
May my mortal blood be spilled.
That my intention be just,
To this Door of Time I entrust.

With a sense of determination, she turned the key, hoping to uncover the secrets hidden in the past.

With a satisfying click, the door swung open, granting Veronica access to the past. She stepped inside the room, then quickly exited, locking the door behind her. Moving to the metal table, she reached underneath and deftly removed the audio player, which had been securely held in place by a strong magnet. Following this meticulous procedure, she also removed the old lock and key from the closet door to erase any trace of her actions in this place.

Veronica spent the rest of the evening connected to the small device with a pair of earbuds. It would take her a week to listen to the entire recording and uncover everything that had been said during that time, but she was hopeful she'd find something incriminating in the beginning.

As she listened, her mind drifted back to her first phone call with Robert when he had called her from his apartment. He had just returned from his trip to Overgaard, Arizona, where he claimed to have received a speeding ticket on the Indian reservation. However, from the conversation on the tape, it seemed he hadn't been entirely truthful with her.

"Yeah, John, I just got back from Vegas, man, and whoa, did I have a line-up of hookers!" Robert's voice came through the recording.

"Wow, you must be a big spender. Did you win a lot?" John's voice replied.

"Oh, yes, at the Blackjack table. You bet! How else do you think I could afford all that fresh meat?!" Robert's tone oozed with boastfulness.

"You're the man, Man!" John's voice responded with enthusiasm.

Veronica couldn't believe what she was hearing. The man she thought she knew seemed to have a hidden side, and she was determined to uncover the truth.

Veronica continued listening to the recorded conversation, feeling a mix of shock and disbelief at the revelations about Robert's intentions.

"I've still got it. And you know, I didn't have to get those hookers; women were coming up to me everywhere. They just seem to gravitate to me. It's usually the chunky girls. I can get any girl with a little meat on her. But I'm getting a little older. I need to settle down. I need to find a payday chick," Robert's voice declared.

Confused, John asked, "What do you mean?"

"A rich chick. Independently wealthy, or who can make me be? My old man said, with my drinking and drugging, he didn't give me past 30, and here I've made it past 50 and I proved him wrong."

John probed further, "Why do you think you've made it?"

"Well, you know I had the surgery, right? Have you seen my picture at 305 pounds?" Robert asked and proceeded to take out his phone to find the picture.

John observed the transformation and commented, "Oh, I see. You look healthy now. So, why do you need a rich chick, then?"

Robert explained, "I need to stop working. I just can't work anymore for the Man. I need to work for myself, or just not work at all, and I need to find a woman to support me. I've never been without a girlfriend for very long. But this time, I am going to be a lot pickier, so I joined this dating site called Zoosk."

Veronica couldn't believe what she was hearing. Robert's motivations seemed driven by financial gain, and she wondered if she had ever truly known the real him. She pondered whether she had found herself in a relationship based on deception and ulterior motives.

Veronica continued to listen, her intrigue growing with every revelation.

"Yes, I'm stringing along 3 of them at the moment, but I'm doing some background checks to see if they are who they say they are," Robert's voice confessed.

Curious, John asked, "By the way, do you say you are who you are? I mean, do you need me to cover for you?"

Robert responded, "Well, John, you're my kind of guy! Yeah, I need you to say I'm from rich parents, which I am. I just don't know if my mom would ever share her money with me! She's so rich, but she's turned into such a miser in her old age that she won't give up a dime. Except for the Indians! She'll donate to every cause—the Indian children, the Leukemia Society, the Alzheimer's Association, the National Cancer Society, you name it. But if it comes to loaning her kids $20 for gas, forget it. She has just turned into a cranky, mean old miser."

John remarked, "Wow. I've never heard anyone talk that way about his mother before."

Robert continued, his voice tinged with sadness, "She didn't used to be that way. Her mother, my grandmother, was the sweetest grandmother alive. She would give you the last $20 bill in her purse, even when she got older and had Alzheimer's. I don't even recognize my mother now. It's really sad."

Veronica couldn't help but sympathize with the complexity of Robert's family dynamics. As she listened to more hours of conversations, she anxiously awaited the next key revelation, hoping to uncover the truth about the man she had fallen in love with.

Veronica continued to listen, her heart sinking as she heard Robert's true intentions revealed.

"I found her! I think I narrowed it down. It's Veronica Frederickson! She comes from a wealthy family, but she's a teacher. She just retired on disability and was knocked out of the will by her sister. And I have a great legal brain. My mom always said I should be a lawyer! And I do love a challenge. I'm going to help her get revenge on her sister, get all that she is owed back, and then have her give it to me!" Robert's voice exclaimed.

"Wow, Rob, you are a crazy conniving con artist, I'll give you that! All power to you, if you can pull that one off!" John responded with admiration.

Veronica's heart sank further as she realized the depth of Robert's deceit. He had been plotting to manipulate her into helping him access her family's wealth. She had given him access to her accounts, and now she felt completely vulnerable.

How long had they been together, and he had already been prying into her will and trying to access her accounts? Only three months? She immediately called her lawyer.

"Cedric Dahl, Attorney at Law. This is his secretary, Jean. How may I help you?" the secretary answered.

"Hi, Jean, Veronica Frederickson here. May I please talk to Mr. Dahl?" Veronica requested it urgently.

"Sure, let me get him on the line," Jean replied.

"Hey, Veronica, how can I help you?" Mr. Calt's voice came through.

"Listen, Mr. Dahl, I'm concerned I may have rushed some decisions about changing my will and power of attorney," Veronica admitted, her voice filled with anxiety.

Veronica felt a mix of relief and worry as she listened to her lawyer's response.

"I'm glad to hear you say that. I was getting ready to give you a call. This guy Robert is a bit shady. I had a background check run on him because he came here the other day and asked for a copy of the Power of Attorney. I thought, 'Why wouldn't he just ask her for a copy?' It was because he didn't want to ask you or didn't want you to know. There's something shady about him. Jean, my secretary, said he was also asking questions about how the power of attorney worked if you were incapacitated. That worried me a little, too," Mr. Dahl revealed.

Veronica's suspicions were confirmed, and she realized that she needed to act swiftly to protect her interests.

The call to her lawyer, the revelations from the tape from the past, and her intuition all pointed to the fact that Robert was not to be trusted.

82

Now, Veronica still had her battle to find the treasure and reclaim her family's long-lost wealth. She knew she had to travel to Tucson to unravel this mystery. With Robert away dealing with his issues on the East Coast, she had a limited window of time to work on her quest before he returned, and she was determined to make the most of it.

Her father had somehow completely disappeared from her life. She was still left with the secret entrance to the basement in Mexico, connecting to the basement in Arizona. However, she had to proceed with caution and avoid getting caught. Her goal was to set up a plan that allowed her to explore the basement from years ago and potentially dig further while she still had that existed in Mexico.

Veronica didn't know how long the basement from her childhood would last there in her Rocky Point House, so she knew she needed to use whatever time she had at her disposal to find any clues to her dad's death. So down she went into the enchanted basement once more, to find out what she could while she could. She took with her her faithful companions Riley, Rudy, and Troubadour, to use their extra special senses in finding things. Dogs were good trackers and could smell things like blood from years ago, which is what Veronica was counting on. She signaled to the three in dog language, "Just find anything that has the scent of blood, drugs, or my father. Here is a piece of his clothing for comparison."

She let the dogs smell her father's shirt and the peach pits he had been eating to ward off cancer to aid in their search of the basement.

As Veronica and the dogs searched the basement, they went through musty, wet cardboard boxes, Veronica opened every book on the bookcase and shook it to make sure there were no papers inside, and the dogs sniffed along every shelf to make sure there were nothing hidden behind the many trinkets, pots, glass, clocks, and statuary housed on them. As Veronica sneezed from the dust stirred up by their movement, Troubadour, Riley, and Rudy all appeared at once with envelopes and bags in their mouths, which they dropped on the floor in front of Veronica, and lay down, exhausted.

"Where did you find these envelopes?"

Riley led the way and showed Veronica a floorboard he clawed at and loosened to reveal a hidden compartment where the dogs had found the envelopes and bag that they had brought her. She then opened the bag, which contained about 30 peach seeds, some of which had been ground down to a powder. The envelopes contained two sets of medical records. One set led to the diagnosis of cyanide poisoning, while the other set, in the other envelope, led to the cause of death being cardiopulmonary complications. She realized that one set of records had been falsified. She also saw that there was a visitor's log, and her sister was the only visitor, besides her mother. These records needed to get into the hands of the police so that the case could be reopened and her sister be brought to justice. She just needed to find someone who could place her sister at the scene of the crime. She needed to find the names of anyone on the hospital records who might have seen her there, or who might have helped her to doctor the records. Then Veronica might be able to find justice for her father. She examined the records, and one name kept coming up. Dr. Reginald Smith. She knew that, if she could get that doctor to turn on her sister, Karina, she would have a case against her. She needed to get all this information, along with a message to this doctor, and to the police to have any chance of re-opening her father's case, since it had been almost 20 years since her father's death, and there had been no murder suspected in the first place. However, the existence of a second autopsy report, written by the same doctor, with an entirely different diagnosis of death would turn some heads. Veronica just had to get these records into the right hands. She sent them to her attorney, and Police Chief Adam Wallace, via mail, but she also sent them through her email, and her an unknown email address, so that anonymously reaching the police, and her sister's contacts at the police department couldn't stop it from getting through.

Patient Name: [Stephen Litchfield]
Medical Record Number: 12509
Date: [December 29.1995]
Attending Physician: Dr. Reginald Smith, MD
Summary: Complaint of Weakness and Fatigue

Chief Complaint: The patient presented complaints of weakness and fatigue, stating that these symptoms have been increasing in severity over the past week.
History: The patient has been battling cancer for several years, with remission noted during the last year.
Physical Examination: Examination revealed general weakness, pallor, and decreased muscle strength. Vital signs within normal range.
Assessment: Weakness and fatigue attributed to cancer-related anemia. Laboratory tests ordered for further evaluation.

Patient Name: [Stephen Litchfield]
Medical Record Number: 125
Date: [December 31.1995]
Attending Physician: Dr. Reginald Smith, MD
Summary: Nausea and Loss of Appetite

Chief Complaint: The patient reported experiencing persistent nausea and a significant loss of appetite over the past two weeks
History: The patient's medical history includes cancer diagnosis and previous rounds of chemotherapy.
Physical Examination: Mild dehydration noted. Abdominal tenderness on palpation.
Assessment: Nausea and loss of appetite attributed to chemotherapy side effects. Hydration and antiemetic medications prescribed.

Patient Name: [Stephen Litchfield]
Medical Record Number: 125
Date: [January 1.1996]
Attending Physician: Dr. Reginald Smith, MD
Summary: Increasing Pain and Fatigue

Chief Complaint: The patient returned, reporting increasing pain, particularly in the abdominal area, and ongoing fatigue.
History: The patient's cancer diagnosis includes metastases to the abdominal region.
Physical Examination: Increased abdominal tenderness and discomfort noted. Fatigue persisting.
Assessment: Pain and fatigue considered indicative of cancer progression. Palliative pain management recommended.

Patient Name: [Stephen Litchfield]
Medical Record Number: 125
Date: [January 2.1996]
Attending Physician: Dr. Reginald Smith, MD
Summary: Continued Symptoms

Chief Complaint: Patient reported no improvement in symptoms. Persistent pain, fatigue, and loss of appetite.
History: The patient's cancer is characterized by its resistance to conventional treatments.
Physical Examination: Unchanged clinical findings.
Assessment: Symptoms consistent with cancer progression. Discussion held with patient and family regarding the limited treatment options available.

Patient Name: [Stephen Litchfield]
Medical Record Number: 125
Date: [January 4,1996]
Attending Physician: Dr. Reginald Smith, MD
Summary: Supportive Care Discussion

Chief Complaint: Patient expressed concerns and distress regarding the worsening symptoms.
History: Patient's cancer has been unresponsive to further chemotherapy options.
Physical Examination: Patient in considerable discomfort, mobility reduced.
Assessment: Given the progression of symptoms and lack of effective treatment options, a discussion was held regarding the transition to palliative care for comfort and symptom management.

Autopsy Report - Case Number: 1996-2467
Deceased: [Stephen Litchfield] DOB: May 4, 1920
Date of Death: [January 6,1996] **Age:** [75] **Gender:** Male
Cause of Death: Cyanide Poisoning
Summary of Findings:

- **External Examination:** The external examination of the deceased revealed no apparent signs of trauma or injury. The body appeared consistent with the reported age.
- **Internal Examination:** The internal examination revealed the presence of excessive cyanide levels in the bloodstream. Cyanide poisoning was determined as the immediate cause of death.
- **Toxicology Report:** A toxicology analysis of the deceased's blood and tissue samples revealed elevated levels of cyanide, consistent with acute poisoning. Additionally, traces of laetrile were detected in the body.
- **Histopathology:** Histopathological examination of organ tissues indicated damage consistent with cyanide exposure, including lesions in the heart and brain.

Discussion:

The presence of cyanide at such elevated levels in the deceased's system is consistent with acute cyanide poisoning. Cyanide is a potent toxic substance that disrupts cellular respiration, leading to rapid death when ingested or absorbed.

The detection of laetrile traces in the body raises suspicion, as laetrile is known to contain amygdalin, which can release cyanide when metabolized. This suggests the possibility that the deceased may have ingested laetrile or a substance containing it.

Based on the findings of this autopsy report, the cause of death for Stephen Litchfield is determined to be cyanide poisoning. Further investigation is recommended to determine the source of cyanide exposure and the circumstances surrounding the ingestion of laetrile.

Autopsy Report 2 - Case Number: 1996-2467
Deceased: [Stephen Litchfield] **DOB:** May 4, 1920
Date of Death: [January 6,1996] **Age:** [75] **Gender:** Male
Cause of Death: Cardiopulmonary Complications

Summary of Findings:
- **External Examination:** The external examination of the deceased revealed no apparent signs of trauma or injury. The body appeared consistent with the reported age.
- **Internal Examination:** The internal examination showed evidence of significant cardiac abnormalities, including severe coronary artery disease and myocardial infarction. Additionally, there were indications of respiratory distress, including pulmonary edema.
- **Toxicology Report:** Toxicology analysis of the deceased's blood and tissue samples revealed the presence of cyanide at elevated levels. Traces of laetrile were also detected.
- **Histopathology:** Histopathological examination of organ tissues indicated damage consistent with chronic heart disease, including extensive fibrosis in the myocardium and pulmonary congestion.

Discussion:
The presence of cyanide in the deceased's system, as revealed by toxicology analysis, is an unexpected finding given the primary cause of death attributed to cardiopulmonary complications. The elevated levels of cyanide could be explained as a result of Mr. Litchfield's unconventional approach to cancer treatment.

Based on the findings of this autopsy report, the primary cause of death for Stephen Litchfield is determined to be cardiopulmonary complications, including severe coronary artery disease and myocardial infarction. The presence of cyanide is noted but attributed to the patient's unorthodox consumption of peach pits containing small amounts of laetrile, a substance known for its controversial use in cancer treatment. Further investigation into the source of cyanide exposure is recommended.

consumption of peach pits containing small amounts of laetrile, a substance known for its controversial use in cancer treatment. Further investigation into the source of cyanide exposure is recommended.

CHAPTER 13

Next, she would need to travel to Tucson to get to know the family living in the house, learn their daily schedule, and when they'd be away. That would be the key to her successful extraction of the treasure.

The only way she could access the basement, cut through the wall, and discover whether there was a hidden room behind it, along with the secret stash of gold bars her father had spoken of, was by going to Tucson and checking out the basement in real time for herself. These gold bars could turn her into a millionaire beyond her wildest dreams. On the other hand, she could choose to dismiss it all as a fantasy, because, otherwise, she would have to tell people how she found out this information, and it would make her look insane.

If she decided to pursue this endeavor, she'd need to overcome the challenge of the house's security system. Figuring out the type of security in place would be crucial. Alternatively, she could explore the legal route of purchasing the house. However, this would involve sharing the secret and potentially losing her fortune, as she didn't have enough money on her own.

Her best course of action was to enlist the help of trustworthy individuals who weren't necessarily wealthy. She knew some people who might be willing to assist her in this venture, as attempting it alone seemed nearly impossible. The challenge lie in identifying those she could genuinely rely on.

However, the most questionable aspect of her plan was explaining how she had obtained the information about the gold bars. Revealing her source could lead to consequences, such as being labeled as delusional or worse. Therefore, she must be discreet and keep this information hidden, as disclosing it could have dire consequences in the eyes of others.

She immediately turned to Google to research alarm systems, with a specific focus on finding out what type of system was installed in the house. This information was crucial for her plan. To gather this intelligence, she realized she needed to obtain a drone. However, her knowledge about drones was limited, so her next task was to educate herself.

Learning was one of her strengths, and she knew how to gather information effectively. She began her online exploration by identifying the primary drone dealers in Southern Arizona. Additionally, she delved into the legal aspects, researching whether drones were permitted in the airspace above Tucson. An important factor to consider was that Tucson housed an Air Force base, which could lead to stricter airspace regulations due to military activity. She needed to ensure her plan wouldn't encounter problems right from the start.

The next step involved distancing herself completely from the operation, making it appear as if she were not involved. This required hiring individuals who were strangers but could be trusted in some way. To accomplish this, she would have to craft a convincing lie that had nothing to do with her original intentions. This lie should provide her with enough time alone in the basement to create an opening in the wall and determine whether her father's claims about hidden gold were true or if it was all a dream. There was also the possibility that her sister had already discovered and removed the gold during the time she lived there alone, even during the remodeling. The only way to know for sure was to investigate the present time.

The enormity of the legwork ahead of her was becoming increasingly apparent, and she had to grapple with the idea that it might not ultimately be worth it. There was even the looming possibility of getting arrested. However, the allure of adventure was too strong to resist, overshadowing these doubts with a sense of excitement.

Yet, there was a persistent shade of doubt casting a gloomy shadow over her thoughts. She pondered whether she should simply continue with her life as it was and find contentment in the role of a teacher who had dedicated 30 years to changing lives. Hadn't she done her part? Wasn't it time to enjoy life, even if that meant entering retirement? But the prospect of retirement felt like slowly fading away, like a form of quiet expiration. It involved taking trips, spending time with family, gardening – all activities that seemed pleasant but didn't answer the question of what she was doing with her life. It felt like a cessation of contribution to society, which was something that she, and people like her, struggled with.

For those who had spent their careers giving to others, the need to continue giving in some capacity persisted. They were the kind of people who couldn't just stop. While some jobs could indeed be detrimental to one's health and needed to be left behind, everyone still required a purpose. The concept of putting anyone on the back shelf seemed inconceivable. She believed that if everyone had a purpose, there might be fewer cases of dementia and Alzheimer's, as the decline of cognitive faculties often occurred when people had nothing to engage their minds.

Her quest led her to visit drone dealerships, only to discover that drones required licenses. To avoid leaving a paper trail, she realized she would need someone else to acquire the license on her behalf. It was a startling realization that she was now thinking and operating like a bona fide criminal. After all, she was planning to break into a house and steal from it, and she had to come to terms with the fact that she had transitioned from being a teacher to becoming a criminal in the pursuit of her quest.

Every criminal has their unique start, a reason that drives them to pursue a life of crime. In Veronica's case, a family member had wronged her, and she sought revenge, aiming to claim what was rightfully hers. Her intention wasn't to cause physical harm; she simply wanted her sister to face the consequences of her greed. Even so, she contemplated the possibility of giving her sister a share if she succeeded in her endeavor. However, she had no intention of revealing the source of the money to Karina, as that would lead to demands for an equal share.

Veronica began her investigation by renting a room at the Sun Ranch, thanks to Robert's careful use of timeshare points. She told him she was visiting her other sister in Tucson, concealing her true intentions. Returning to the old neighborhood near El Cid Mall, La Posada, brought a flood of memories. It was a pleasant place to grow up, with a prominent circle of cacti, ocotillo, and small wildlife at its center. Her childhood home was unmistakable, surrounded by a lush garden of palm trees her father had planted and a protective line of oleander bushes guarding the front. Her father had planted a row of rose bushes to pick a fresh rose for her mother every morning. As she passed the half-moon gravel drive, all these memories rushed back to her.

Veronica had a clear plan for finding out who currently resided in her childhood home. Her method involved accessing their mailbox, a black wrought iron box with a flip-top lid. All she needed was a piece of their mail to extract a name. Once she had a name, she could initiate her online investigation using tools like Google People Finder, Facebook, and more. It was her way of gaining insights into the people currently living in the house and, potentially, their schedule.

Veronica uncovered the story through a combination of methods. Initially, she learned about the wife's family background and high-society connections by accessing the mailbox's contents. Names from the mail allowed her to conduct online searches using platforms like Google People Finder, Facebook, and others to gather more information.

Veronica discovered that Darlene and Steve McGregor were the ones who had purchased the property from her sister in 2014. Armed with this information, she delved into social media platforms like Facebook, Instagram, LinkedIn, and YouTube, eager to learn more about them. Her mission was to determine their vacation patterns and identify windows of opportunity for a successful plan. As she continued, she couldn't help but notice how her thought process was shifting, taking on a more cunning and criminal edge. Surprisingly, she found herself embracing this transformation.

Her research revealed that the couple had two older teenagers attending private high schools, one college student, and a Pekinese dog named Ruffles. They seemed to come from old money, with a summer home in the Hamptons, Long Island. Steve, the husband, had been a New York stockbroker who had eventually burnt out in the city. He sold his New York house and moved his family to Arizona, near his parents. It appeared that he had cashed out, with the price tag of their current home being a modest $800,000 compared to their previous $2 million residence.

Veronica delved deeper into her research, uncovering the wife's maiden name, Darlene Bennington. It became evident that Darlene Bennington had been born into a high-society family, and she had hosted lavish parties with the crème de la crème of society, serving the most extravagant cuisine in the finest venues. However, her life took a different turn when she married the man her family disapproved of and moved out west, far from their upscale world. This decision tarnished her mother's reputation, and it was a topic of constant discussion at every gathering.

Tilly, Darlene's mother, faced the criticism with grace, thanks to her husband, Grandpa Joe. He defended Darlene and her husband, Steven, noting that he was a gentleman who had moved west to prioritize family time over his career, ultimately saving their marriage. He admonished those who cared solely about money and gossip.

Despite the distance, Darlene made an effort to bring her children back east to visit her parents as frequently as possible. She missed the luxurious lifestyle that wealth afforded her. Veronica found this out by getting into her email account and noting the number of emails discussing trips back to the Hamptons, along with the accompanying airline receipts.

In Veronica's numerous drone footage takes of the house, along with her eyewitness accounts, under cover of her invisibility cloak, she learned that, occasionally, Darlene would retreat to the basement and open the safe, adorning herself with stunning jewelry: 23-carat earrings and a necklace with 20 23-carat diamonds, a tiara, bracelets, pins, and various rings. She would wander through the house, admiring her collection of priceless artworks, where their true wealth lay. In these moments, she would turn up the music and dance around, imagining herself at a cotillion ball back east among her mother's affluent friends, reconnecting with her high society roots. She was able to time these events to take place, coincidently, on the night of her husband's poker games, Thursday nights at 5 pm. Interestingly enough, the kids all had appointments or sports at that time, as well, so the only person scheduled to be in the house was Mrs. Darlene McGregor.

Mrs. McGregor's aspiration was for her children to embrace their Bennington heritage and the upper echelons of high society, believing that they were destined for greatness. She was determined that her children would not face early pregnancies, forsake their college careers, or compromise their dreams, as she had. Instead, she envisioned them becoming doctors, lawyers, politicians, and, most importantly, college graduates.

As Veronica observed her old house during a drive-by, Veronica noticed two cars in the driveway for the guesthouse, indicating the presence of renters. She made sure to check their names through the mailbox's mail contents, as well. The renters, she found out, were nonexistent. She went to look in the rental and it was cleaned out. Nothing was in the fridge, but a few beers. The bed was made, but there were no clothes in the closet or drawers. There were 3 books on the shelf. Therefore, what they had done was smart; they parked two cars in the back, making it appear that there were renters in the back while they were gone so that thieves like her would be deterred from breaking in!

Veronica's ultimate goal, with all this research, was to identify a time when the family would be away for an extended period, granting her the opportunity to enter the house, cut a hole in the wall, and potentially find the gold without being detected.

The next crucial step Veronica planned was to identify trustworthy individuals. The people aspect of the plan was delicate and required careful consideration. To ensure that no one would cheat her or run away with her money, she needed to truly understand the people she would involve. This posed a significant challenge: should she disclose the true purpose of her involvement, or should she gather more information about the family living in the house and see if they had anything of value to steal? Perhaps making it seem like they were there to steal an alternate valuable item was the way to go.

Though Veronica acknowledged that handling heavy gold bars alone would be a challenge and she would likely require assistance, she decided it would be wiser to disclose only the existence of the diamonds to him, for fear it would put at risk her entire family fortune. She decided it would be wisest to just find out if the gold existed, to only take a few bars, and come back for the rest later. She wondered if offering him a substantial share might convince him to join her, but knew that his aspirations for wealth would overshadow any reason, and he would just take it all.

She was trying to determine whether the main house had a security system like Ring or another surveillance system. Veronica realized that it might be possible to discreetly attach her security system alongside theirs without arousing suspicion. Accessing the device through wifi was another possibility. But she also knew that enlisting professional hackers to assist in gaining access to the security system's account, allowing her to navigate the house's security, would be a better bet. She was not a professional hacker. Veronica recognized that her lover, Robert, had connections with individuals who possessed the necessary skills for this task, even if they were on the wrong side of the law. However, trusting Robert to uphold his end of the bargain seemed uncertain.

Therefore, Veronica knew she needed a plan B, as she couldn't rely on Robert to remain loyal throughout the endeavor. Her quest for trustworthy assistance would continue as she prepared to move forward with her plan to uncover the secrets hidden within her childhood home. When Robert turned on her or stole from her, she would still be able to go back and get the family gold. That was her Plan B. She got a satchel that had a false bottom, so she could hide whatever she found in the false bottom.

Veronica had devised a Plan B. Now it involved reaching out to her boyfriend, Robert, to enlist his assistance. She made a call, adopting a friendly tone.

"Robert? It's so good to hear your voice. I'm in Oro Valley, at your favorite place, Sun Ranch. I miss your arms around me. How was the graduation?"

Robert replied, venting his frustrations about the graduation, particularly regarding his mother's boyfriend and a heated family argument.

Veronica offered her perspective on the situation, calling the boyfriend dumb and sharing her bewilderment at her mother's choice. Robert continued to share the chaos of the evening, with his daughters getting into a fight during his daughter Alexandra's graduation celebration.

Veronica empathized, remarking on the catfight. Then, she presented her proposal to Robert.

"Well, Veronica, do you want me to meet you in Tucson, then? How long do you need to stay there?"

"I have something to take care of here, that I need your help with, and it may take a few weeks."

Robert agreed to her request and offered to fly to Tucson in two days, expressing his love for her. Veronica reciprocated the sentiment, sealing the deal for her Plan B with the hope that her boyfriend could provide valuable assistance in her upcoming endeavor.

As Veronica drove to the Tucson International Airport to pick up Robert, memories of her father's stories about Tucson's real estate history flooded her mind. He had shared how Tucson was once divided in the real estate market during the 1970s, with Broadway acting as the dividing line. North of Broadway was North Tucson, while South Tucson was south of the line. Her father had recounted how he was discouraged from showing houses north of Broadway to Mexican-Americans in those times, an injustice he felt compelled to oppose. He had even left the firm that gave him those instructions, demonstrating his integrity and conviction.

Veronica admired her father greatly, seeing him as a role model for standing up for what he believed was right. She aspired to emulate his principles.

Upon Robert's arrival at the airport, Veronica greeted him with humor, playfully inviting him into the car.

"Robert, come on and get in," she gestured with one hand towards the passenger seat while trying to be funny.

Robert chuckled and responded,

"First-class service, I see."

Instead of taking the offered seat, he surprised her by pulling her into his arms and planting a long, passionate kiss on her lips. There was no resistance from her; it felt surprisingly romantic, and Robert's scent, the familiar Armani fragrance, awakened a long-forgotten attraction. At that moment, Veronica simply melted into his embrace.

Veronica was acutely aware of the hold that Robert had over her, and she recognized the need to regain control of the situation. As they drove back to the timeshare together, she resolved to maintain a facade of normalcy.

CHAPTER 14

Veronica began by sharing some information with Robert, emphasizing that the current residents of the house were wealthy and possessed a significant collection of jewels. Veronica proposed a partnership, suggesting they collaborate on a heist and split the proceeds. She offered to divide the profits between them, depositing a portion in his bank account and keeping the rest in hers.

With this approach, Veronica aimed to maintain the appearance of a straightforward arrangement while secretly harboring her agenda. She hoped that by presenting the plan in a way that appealed to Robert's interests, she could navigate the situation with more control and discretion.

Robert said he did know people who could hack computers, people who could fly drones, safe crackers, and house robbers, so all the people needed for the job. But he was going to have to find out what cuts these people would want and bring them together.

Veronica and Robert began assembling their team for what was shaping up to be a high-stakes heist. The first member was Freddie, Delilah's son and a computer whiz kid. To get Freddie on board, Robert would have to pretend to break up with Veronica and reunite with Delilah, all while secretly planning to pretend to work with Veronica on the heist, and then turn on her. The plan was to convince Freddie to join the operation. Robert would then arrange for Veronica's share to be delivered to her discreetly, two days later when the coast was clear. But two days later, the rest of the team had cleared out, leaving Veronica with nothing.

Next on the team was Val, one of Robert's ex-girlfriends who had experience as both a bank robber and a safecracker. Her skills would prove invaluable for the heist.

The final member was a former crew supervisor from Robert's time working in New Jersey as a collection agent for a construction company. Vince Verducci had experience in similar operations and was known for being tough. Robert's ability to assemble such a crew highlighted his expertise in orchestrating heists.

Veronica was aware that she was embarking on a risky endeavor and needed to play her cards carefully. Her secret magical ability was her one unique advantage, and she pondered how she could leverage it. She knew she couldn't reveal her secret to Robert or the rest of the team, as it could be used against her.

The road ahead was filled with uncertainty and danger, and Veronica was determined to navigate it as cautiously as possible.

Step one of their plan involved staging a fake break-up, which turned out to be an unexpectedly enjoyable experience for both Robert and Veronica. They orchestrated a dramatic scene in a well-known restaurant, pretending to slap each other and acting as though they were parting ways. This performance was captured on video and uploaded to YouTube, causing Veronica's sons to become concerned. They reached out to her, expressing their worries and reminding her that they had warned her about Robert. Veronica assured them they were right and told them she was planning to visit them soon but needed some time to recover from the breakup with a spa vacation in Tucson. Her sons supported the idea and even sent her money to enhance her trip.

Meanwhile, Robert returned to Pennsylvania and successfully wooed his old girlfriend, Delilah, convincing her to get back together with him. His smooth-talking skills played a crucial role in rekindling their romance. Delilah and her computer whiz son, who was always at her side, began preparing to visit Arizona for a getaway within a week.

Robert explained to Delilah his past involvement with Veronica and revealed that he believed she could be the key to a fortune. He proposed that they could cash in on this opportunity, utilizing her son's computer skills, intelligence, and the expertise of a few other talented individuals he knew. It was a tantalizing proposition, and Robert's charm seemed to be working its magic once again.

"Tell me the plan, and I'll tell you what I think."

Robert began describing Veronica as "a crazy, jealous woman who wouldn't stop crying about how her sister had gotten more than her in her parents' will." She was "stalking the house where she grew up," even though "strangers lived there now!"

"I'm pretending to still date her so that she will think I am agreeing to plan a robbery of the house she used to live in, to appease her. I'm going to tell her that I am pretending to date you, just to be able to use your son's abilities. Then gather the other team members as well, to pull off this job. Of course, they are all ex-girlfriends. What can I say?"

"Figures," Delilah chuckled, "So am I going to regret this?"

"Not when you see how much money you will make from your piece of the pie." Robert had graduated from the Dale Carnegie *How to Win Friends and Influence People* Course. A salesman through and through, he could sell ice to the Eskimos. His mom had wanted him to be a lawyer, but he was never sent to a four-year college like his younger brother. He had just gotten into too much trouble for smoking pot. Therefore, he went to restaurant management school, and he knew how to manage people and businesses. He had a head for law, real estate, finance. He had done sales in all three, as well as mortgages, real estate, banking, stocks, electronics, construction, and labor. He knew a lot, but he didn't have the certificates to prove it until you talked to him. Then you knew he was a man that knew what he was talking about. He had used his salesmanship and lawyer qualities, along with his notable womanizing skills, in making the case for Delilah and her son to be in on the robbery.

Now it was time to somehow convince Robert's ex-girlfriend, Val, to join them. Val had the gift of being able to crack any safe and open any lock, door, window, or drawer. You name it, she could get into it. You would think that with a reputation like that, she would be famous, right? But no, she tried to stay undercover. Her skills were widely sought after, so she had to be on the move all the time. It was very difficult to maintain a relationship with someone who was always moving. That's why Robert didn't stay with her; he couldn't keep up with her exciting yet transient lifestyle. She was always on the run.

However, Val was quite smitten with Robert, it turned out, so anytime he texted "potential safe job" to the last number she had given him, she showed up, but not always on time. Because they were on the clock, they needed to find her sooner rather than later. Robert tried to triangulate where he had last met up with her and the last two times he had met her, but that didn't make her any easier to locate. This was going to require some assistance from Veronica and her dog, Riley.

Val was a real dog lover, and the way to her heart was through cute, furry little creatures. So, to entice her, perhaps a dog could get locked in a safe, and word could go out through the safe-cracking community. Time was running out, and a dog's life was in danger. It involved a big reward, and Riley was willing to be the dog. Veronica was at the scene when she came to rescue her. The safe owner was relieved and paid the money, but it was kept a private affair to keep her identity secure. Veronica made a promise to write her biography, and she loved the idea, coming to a meeting at the timeshare where the robbery plan was hatched.

The final team member was one of the collection agents from the construction company where Robert used to work. He was still in New Jersey, a tough guy who could help drive and be a lookout and knew how to plan and execute robberies. Robert was flying him in. Despite being in his seventies now, when he got off the plane and Veronica saw him, he towered over her like a Redwood. His arms were as big as his head, and his muscles popped out of the white Steelers t-shirt he'd squeezed into. His name was not one that many would speak out loud- Vito Vigalucci. He was a made man, not someone you would mess with, as Robert had warned Veronica. He had several deaths on his record; he had been a hitman for the mob.

CHAPTER 15

I
t had all led to this. Veronica knew that the whole rest of her life would be determined by what happened on this one night. It had to all go as planned, or else. The team was to rendezvous at the El Cid Mall shopping center parking lot, parking near the wall to the neighborhood in the Walco parking lot. Veronica knew that Riley could be a strategic ally in this endeavor. She asked Riley to stick close by Val during the heist, since she had already had an encounter with Val before, and "be her eyes and ears." Therefore, Riley knew what was happening and could inform Veronica when trouble was afoot.

As Veronica thought back, she recalled her childhood days when she and her friends used to slip through the one little fence that had a pretty big gap in it near Williams' house. She parked near the spot where it was supposed to be, and sure enough, it was still there.

As she waited for the other team members to arrive, being back in the old neighborhood caused Veronica to be whisked away in her thoughts.

It was her 13th birthday party when her mother gave every one of her friends $5 and sent them on a scavenger hunt to the mall. They all walked in pairs over to the mall in a big group. Whoever could get the most items

107

for their $5 would win all the items that were purchased. The most creative ideas were the winners. The winner couldn't get all the same items either, like 10 of something. It was a lot of fun, and in those days, a dollar went a lot further. There was also a time limit, so the girls had to be back at the house within 90 minutes. Veronica looked back on that party with laughter. It was the one time in school when she actually felt kind of popular.

Middle school had been the only time she had a boyfriend. She'd been bullied in elementary school and felt somewhat out of place in high school, but middle school had been kind of magical because of George Gray. He was on the basketball team, and she was a manager for the volleyball team. There had been a plane crash near the school, and everyone was evacuated to the cafeteria. He had come up to her and asked her if she was okay. From that day forward, in seventh grade through eighth grade, they had dated. George was her first real love, and it took a long time to get over him.

She had been going to her old neighborhood for a few weeks now, meticulously mapping out the back alleys that were the easiest to navigate and drawing a detailed map. This brought back memories of getting in trouble with her neighbors for spying on their backyards when she and her friends used to run through the alleys as kids.

Veronica had to be much more stealthy and under the radar about it this time because she didn't live in the neighborhood anymore. This time, it wasn't fun and games; she was a stranger, planning to rob the place—a criminal who, if caught, would go to jail.

They all had practiced the route to the house and back, timing it several nights in a row. Even Freddie, the computer whiz kid that he was, asked to practice turning off the security once before the official night, just to make sure he could. They had him come along once and turn it off. It didn't work the first time, so it was a good thing it was a practice run. The next night, he tried again and realized it was all due to using the wrong username.

He had used his old username instead of the one he should have. He didn't notice the mistake until the next day when he went into the security system and saw that it had saved his credentials with his username. He changed the username to the owner's username, and it worked, of course! And they were in!

The plan was to rob the house when the owners were away, but finding out the location of everything in the house might require several trips. Though the family was away on Long Island for a while, they had to return home for school, so the new pest control company plan was devised to get the family out of the house for a few hours, while the basement was bombed for cockroaches. It would be difficult to accomplish this all in one night, unless they had a lot of time, or could distract the owners from paying attention to the goings-on in the basement. First, Robert would come and get the mother to agree to have the company come in with a terrific special they couldn't say no to. They would come in several times in between, when the family was to be away on vacation, to learn about the layout of the house. Then, when they returned from vacation, as set up by the husband, on the day of the treatment, they would pull off the robbery.

The map led them through the alleys behind the Williams' house. Pete Williams, who had been in Veronica's class in school, had made sure to direct all his friends to "throw above the waist" in dodgeball when she was on the opposing side. 5th graders could be so cruel. Of course, later, when she returned from college on Christmas break, at the neighborhood Christmas party at the O'Reilly's, she would get her silent revenge when he asked her on a date to go down to Nogales for the day.

Veronica got in his car, and to her dismay, he had such a horrible body odor that she could hardly stand it. She never went out with him again. Pete had gotten his just reward for bullying her - he stunk!

These alleyways were nothing like the New Jersey pits with aluminum cans, the stench of molding lasagna, and port wine behind the Italian restaurants that Vince Verducci was used to. Instead, the fragrance of fruit trees, wildflowers, roses, and hibiscus wafted through the oleander walls that most of the homes had, along with their stucco walls and wrought iron gates.

The most elaborate of gardens was to be found next door at the Duff's house. They were so well-known for their gardens that there was a constant line of cars driving through the neighborhood just to see their front yard. The team had to slip by very discreetly because there were always people about. A gardening crew was required to keep the property looking well-groomed, and they would use the entourage of cars to their advantage.

When Robert pulled up in his pest control van, he would have been seen coming and going by all the people in the line of cars, and they would be able to back his story. However, the line of cars wasn't as easily traversed for those on foot. So, Robert made a quick stop, pretending to make a sales call at the Duff house, which he expected to get rejected. He approached the red door with a white column on either side guarding the house, resembling one of the Queen's guards, and rang the doorbell.

He had backed up the van so that the back doors were not visible from the front door of the house and got his clipboard out of the back. Then he left the back door slightly ajar. As soon as he walked up to the house and when the coast was clear, the rest of the crew bolted from the back alley where they had been hiding and quietly hid in the back of the van, closing the door very discreetly.

"Hello. What do you want?" the intercom squawked, making Robert jump. He hadn't seen the intercom next to him on the white column.

"Hello. Is the man or woman of the house available? I'm here from Johnson Pest Control to ask if you'd like pest control service," he pushed the intercom button to say.

"We're all set. No thanks. Goodbye."

"No worries. Have a nice day, ma'am," he charmingly accepted defeat and returned to his vehicle. But really, he had won. He had managed to get his team in the vehicle without anyone noticing.

Next stop, the Blakes' house, which was across the street. Yes, their eldest daughter, Eloisa, used to babysit Veronica when she was little. They were my dearest friends. It was one of those tan

Santa Fe Adobe houses with log poles sticking out, two stories tall. Robert had to stop there to let them out, as it was across the street, on the corner. Once again, he went up to the front door, and in the meantime, the crew immediately disappeared out the back door of the van. It was a quick rejection, and he was back in the van. The Blakes had moved up to Phoenix long ago.

A new generation of strangers was taking over the old neighborhood. Veronica wondered if this was the way it always felt for people as they grew older. The new people moved in as the older people died and moved out. A new generation might not even know who lived in their homes and the stories that took place there unless someone decided to write them down.

Their next move was across the street. They just had to get across and behind the Sturge's white brick house, with the balcony that ran across the second floor. Veronica, of course, knew Mrs. Sturges. Her son's construction company had built much of Tucson, but what she remembered most was that she had had Barry Goldwater over when he was running for office.

Even Veronica's mother had been the President of the Pima County Republican Women's Association. In college, she remembered the phone calls during election time.

"Now, Roni, I have mailed your absentee ballot to your mailbox. Don't forget to vote Republican!"

"Mom, I promise I will vote, but I am not going to tell you how I vote."

"Well, that's fine, but there's only one choice. You'll see. I've sent you the editorial showing you who you should vote for, so you'll know who to vote for."

"Thanks, Mom." She gave up, knowing it was no use to arguing, and better to just agree and get off the phone, and then vote how she wanted anyway.

The Sturges were right next door, with a row of ornamental orange trees in the alley between the two houses. The terrible taste of orange soup came to mind when she saw them. Her father had tried to make the ornamental oranges edible, not just ornamental. He boiled them into a soup and asked us all to try it. It was, of course, disgusting! Her dad just couldn't stand the idea that the fruit couldn't be used for something.

Finally, they had reached their destination. To ensure the guesthouse renters were not there, they had received an all-expenses-paid trip to Florida. The guesthouse had been empty for the last week and would be until the following week. The security system was hacked by Pete, the computer genius.

Robert, posing as the pest control salesman, seized his moment. He went over the specifics of today's roach bombing with the husband, who, distracted by his wife's dancing around wearing all her good diamonds, signed off on & agreed to everything without suspicion, while the uniformed team members filed in with their equipment, down into the basement.

"You will need to stay out of the basement for 24 hours."

Meanwhile, the rest of the team readied themselves for the "pesticide bombing" Robert, the charismatic leader, knew that the new family living in Veronica's childhood home had diamonds stashed away. Veronica had led them to believe they were just here to steal those diamonds, but Veronica had her agenda in mind.

As Robert briefed the team, he glanced at Veronica, who seemed lost in thought.

"Veronica, are you with us?" he asked.

She snapped back to attention.

"Of course, Robert. I'm ready."

Upstairs, in the lavish living room of the house, the husband believed his diamonds were secure in the hidden safe behind a bookcase in the basement. Little did he know, his wife had a different idea. She had taken out the diamond jewelry and was dancing around the house, reveling in the memory of her rich family heritage that she had married out of.

Outside, Vito Verducci, the seasoned driver from New Jersey, kept a close eye on the surroundings. His sharp senses were finely tuned to detect any suspicious activity. He'd be the first to warn the team if anything went awry.

Back in the basement, Pete, Delilah's computer whiz son, was hard at work disabling the security system. With nimble fingers, he breached the digital defenses, allowing the team to move forward.

Veronica knew the layout of the basement like the back of her hand. She discreetly guided the team toward the safe with the diamonds in it. She directed Riley to stay with the other team members, and listen in on their conversations, while Veronica slunk away to find the wall her father had spoken of. Veronica had always been a teacher, but today she found herself in a very different role. In the dimly lit basement of her childhood home, she kneeled, tools in hand, ready to cut a hole in the wall. Her father's ghostly voice had whispered secrets of hidden gold bars, and she was determined to find them. With precision, she began cutting a hole. She only had enough time to cut a hole big enough for her arm to fit through. As the team moved swiftly, Vito's keen eye caught a neighbor's suspicious glance. He acted fast, sending a subtle signal to the others. Robert wrapped up his sales pitch, ensuring the husband would remain occupied.

Veronica's hands trembled as she cut through the final layer of the wall. She reached inside and gasped in disbelief. Gold bars, just as her father had promised, gleamed in the dim light. She grabbed only two, due to their weight, tucked them into the false bottom of her satchel, and joined the others.

"Where have you been?" Delilah asked.

"I just get so caught up in the memories of this place, I forget the time," was her excuse.

"That's all we need is a daydreamer to get us caught!" Val said.

The team moved quickly. They found the book in the bookcase that had to be tipped forward to unlatch the moveable bookcase. Then they found the safe behind it. Val, the safecracker, stepped forward and put on her gloves. Her hands expertly twisted the lock, listening with her stethoscope. The safe clicked open, revealing the glittering diamonds inside. Val handed the real diamonds to Veronica, who put them in the satchel she had brought for this purpose. Then Delilah handed her the identical fake ones, one at a time, putting them back in the same positions they were in to avoid suspicion. Once they had all the real diamonds in their possession, they closed the safe and the bookcase's false front, and retreated, leaving no trace of their intrusion. However, some of the most valuable diamonds were still dancing around the house, on the person of Mrs. McGregor! Because the basement was bombed for cockroaches and the family couldn't access the safe that night, the diamonds couldn't be returned to the safe. So, the diamonds would have to be kept out of the safe. Veronica knew about the wife's crazy dancing with diamonds fetish, so she had planned ahead of time for the phenomenon. She had Robert leave the husband with a complimentary pen from Johnson Pest Control, which, of course, had a covert microphone inside of it so they could hear the goings-on inside of the house after they had gone. He made sure to give one to the wife as well, saying to pass them on to her friends. Therefore, they were privy to this conversation:

"What has gotten into you? Why are you wearing your diamonds around the house?"

"Well, you never take me anywhere that I can wear them like I could back home. Why is that? Why can't we go to the opera? Or to the Country Club parties? The people in this neighborhood do. Don't you want our kids to grow up thinking they are successful."

"Yes, but you are just acting plain batty. People are beginning to talk!"

"Oh, they're just jealous!"

"Please put your jewels in this box in my dresser until I can take them down to the safe in the morning. I will take you to the opera if that's what you want, but stop acting like a loon, so our children aren't just embarrassed!"

"I guess you're right. I don't want that. But will you take me?"

"Yes, I promise."

"I love you."

"Now, let's get ready for dinner. We're going over to Sheila and

Jim's in the Foothills. I know it's only casual, but we can have a good time; no diamonds needed."

"Okay."

That was the cue for the team. They were able to drive over to the mall, stay there, and then make it back through the neighborhood silently on foot, through the alleyways once more. This time, only Freddie was needed to break through the security system, and Vito to climb up the back wall near the living room, silently scale his way over to the bedroom window, and jimmy the lock on the window. Then, get the jewels, replace them with the fakes, and back out. There was just one little discrepancy. When he got to the window, it wasn't the regular kind that you can go under with a blade and flip, so they had to get Val to come and try the lock. She got through the neighborhood and came to the living room window.

"Maybe we should try to get along differently," Val said.

"Okay, I'm game," Vito replied.

"Let's try the kitchen door, or this side door."

Sure enough, the side door was the weak link in the security of the house. It had just been added at the last minute when Veronica's mom needed to be moved downstairs because she had Alzheimer's and her sister had to move in. The addition was made from wood and wood doors, not brick and stucco. It was clear that her sister had gotten the lowest bid to do the work. The door was easily broken into as a result of the poor workmanship. It was also clear that the security system wasn't even included in this section of the building. Val tested the door, and her simple hairpin in the lock did the trick; they were in. She and Vito were up to the master bedroom in a flash, replacing the fake jewels with the real ones - 2 necklaces, earrings, 4 bracelets, tiara, and 3 rings - which the wife had been flaunting around the house. Then they got out of there, again through the little patio door. They made sure to leave everything in the house the same as when they went in. They sped back through the alley to the awaiting van, where Veronica had the jewels in her satchel.

However, they didn't want to leave all the jewels in just one person's possession. There was a concern about fairness among the lot. So, when they got to the van, each of them took a necklace, a pair of earrings, several bracelets, and 2 rings. They were each to get in their separate vehicles, take off their black robbery clothes, re-park, and find their way to the Walco, where they would go shopping for some party snacks and all leave together, meet at their cars, and drive back to the timeshare. Delilah and Freddie would follow Robert to "dump" the van at a friend's house, where he'd pull the "Johnson Family Pest Control" sticker off the back and sides of the Terminix van, and jump into Delilah's vehicle to join everyone at the timeshare.

The house's new occupants remained blissfully unaware, Mr. McGregor thinking only of the extravagant diamond jewelry dancing in the hands of his wife, and wondering how he was ever going to measure up to her family heritage.

Veronica, back in her SUV, gazed down through the sparkling diamonds at the glint of the gold bars where she had partially unzipped the false bottom of her satchel, a mix of emotions washing over her. She had found her father's treasure, but she was only able to carry two of the heavy bars. Her father had left her more gold than she had ever imagined. This was going to make her rich beyond her dreams, but she had that funny feeling come over her, the kind she got when things were just not right. She knew something was wrong, but she couldn't figure it out. Veronica knew she'd better be on guard and hide these as soon as possible.

Back at the timeshare, when everyone had arrived, the champagne bottles popped. The team celebrated their successful heist.

"Here's to Veronica!" Delilah was the first to say.

"Yes, I agree. You had the idea," Robert said.

"Thanks, but you made it happen," Veronica said.

"Yes, but even an old-timer can see that it took your knowledge of all the details to get us here!" Vito agreed.

"Here, here!" Val said.

"Here's to Veronica!" Freddie said.

"And to all of you," Veronica replied.

And the toasting of each other and drinking kept going into the night.

CHAPTER 16

When Veronica woke up in the morning, she felt very hazy. It wasn't morning; it was more like afternoon. She leaned over and looked at her cell phone next to her bed and saw that it was not only afternoon; it was the afternoon of the next day! She had slept an entire day away. Was she that tired? No. Had she been drugged? She started looking around the timeshare; there was no one else there. No one else's things were there. They had cleared out their things and taken off! They had planned to go, but she was supposed to wake up, and they were supposed to split everything. She looked for her satchel that she had tucked away in the closet. She saw it was still there, but she picked it up. It was significantly lighter.

They had found the gold bars! Oh no!

When it was nearing dusk, she quickly got her things together got in her car, and drove down to her old neighborhood, parked near the Walco, and started through the alleyways, practically running through her mapped route. When she reached her house, instead of going the way she had given to her team, she chose another route, through the window well that led down to the basement.

She wished she had used it to sneak in and out at night when

119

she was in high school, but she was always too goody-two-shoes for that. It was an easy entrance, except for the black windows, so she just took her flat-headed screwdriver and slid it under the glass door near the lock, the latch moved, and the door opened. She had to squeeze a bit to fit in the small square of glass to get in, but, fortunately, she had lost enough weight, and she could do it.

Veronica was in her basement once again, but this time, she had a very negative feeling. She went to the hole she had cut, which had been cut bigger. Robert and the rest of the team had double-crossed her. She had not told them everything; it's true. But she put her head through the hole, which now could fit, and she could see that they had taken it all. Every last bar. Her hopes for everlasting funds were no longer in reach. The lost gold was lost again. She was never going to be able to claim her family in history or gain wealth herself. It was just a sad state of affairs.

The only thing she could think to do was to reach out to Robert and appeal to his feelings for her. Perhaps he had some kind of empathy for her situation. Maybe if she just understood the history of her family and the importance the gold played in her family's history. Robert didn't know the history behind it. Of course, her call went straight to voicemail.

"Robert, if you cared about me at all, I just want you to know that that gold is the Lost Confederate Gold. There's more about it that you need to know before you just go pawn it."

Almost immediately, his name came up on her screen.

"That got your interest, I see."

"Why did you keep this from me? From us?" She heard the others mumbling in the background.

"It was my family's heritage. I didn't want to give it all away. I want to report it to the historical society and get my family's history registered as those who were associated with saving the gold. It was the Lost Confederate Gold of the Civil War. It had been en route to Richmond, Virginia, and one of its wagons was blasted in a battle near Baltimore. Some Confederate soldiers had it, but they died along the route. My great-grandfather happened to be traveling back to his hometown outside of Baltimore. He found the load to hide the Confederate Gold at Twin Oaks in the Carriage House."

"So then how did it get all the way here to Arizona?"

"It was kept safe there for years until my dad moved West to Arizona. Then he sealed it in a room in his basement and waited for a family member he knew he could trust with such a secret." Veronica added.

"Well, why didn't he tell you this long ago when he was alive? Why didn't you get it then?"

She knew that he was setting her up, but she said anyway, "He died before he could reveal the secret to me because my sister, Karina poisoned him."

"Oh, I see. And how do you know this?"

"He came back as a ghost and told me."

"Now you're seeing ghosts? Maybe you should see a therapist."

Veronica hung up on him, sensing where this was headed. Staying with him meant risking commitment to an institution, giving him full control over her life. What she hadn't realized was that he had been using her phone's location to track her the entire time they were on the call. She looked up just in time to see a blurry figure resembling Robert and felt a needle prick her arm.

CHAPTER 17

Hours later, she woke up in a sterile, white hospital room, her wrists and ankles tightly bound. Robert had seized upon her "seeing ghosts" claim to have her committed. How he had managed this feat she could only guess—perhaps he'd even involved her sister. Yet Veronica maintained enough clarity of thought to realize that her best course of action was to behave sanely. If she screamed or acted out, they'd likely medicate her into submission. The calmer and more rational she acted, the sooner she would regain her freedoms.

Over the next few days, as she displayed increasing rationality, she earned more liberties within the hospital. Veronica began to befriend the staff and inquired about her whereabouts. Realizing she had to take action to escape, her thoughts turned to lessons from her father. She needed a closet! Could she manifest changes in any closet? Why not try? She started jotting down what needed to happen, contemplating a chant that could bring about these changes. Confidence was key; she had to believe in the chant's power. Practicing the words became her next step, but her drugged state initially hampered her memory. It took her a week to clear her head sufficiently to make her move.

The most effective approach, she realized, was to alter the

course of history. Now she had to consider what needed altering. Robert simply knew too much. She had to go back to a pivotal moment and find a way to change it. What was the key event that, if altered, could reshape her life's direction at this point? She concluded that if Robert had never discovered the gold bars, things might have been different. Ideally, she should have waited to cut the hole leading to the gold bars until she was alone; this would have eliminated any motive for betrayal. And she certainly wouldn't have mentioned her father's ghost to Robert—a glaring mistake on her part.

To rewrite history, Veronica needed to find a closet in that basement, obtain a key and a lock, and execute her "procedure," as she had come to call it. By altering that single event, she could unlock a different future for her family.

In retrospect, she had indeed pulled off the entire heist and secured the gold bars. She could have returned for the rest undetected if they hadn't discovered those initial four bars. Once she found the basement, she had to obtain a key. She had seen one man who had an affinity for old relics, so she started to visit his room regularly and ask him to tell her stories about history. She finally caught a glimpse of an old key he had in his drawer and asked if he could borrow it for the day, just as a show-and-tell item for another friend. Then she would return it to him. He obliged, no questions asked. Veronica made her way to the basement and worked on changing the course of history to not include going after any of the gold so that the whereabouts of the gold bars would never be revealed to the scoundrels with whom she had pulled off the robbery. She wrote down her plan on paper. Then began her chant.

> *Lock of old, key of gold;*
> *Let us change the story told,*
> *When we right the family gold.*
> *Grant us time upon this date*
> *To open up this hourly gate.*

If our intention should be ill,
May our mortal blood be spilled.
That our intention be just,
To the Door of Time, we entrust.
You know my intention to be just;
Door of Time, only to me entrust.

Veronica woke up alone in the timeshare the morning after the robbery, just as she had before. This time, however, she found that Robert had taken her share of the diamonds from her satchel. Once again, the rest of the team had vanished from the timeshare. Unlike before, however, she didn't bother calling him; she wanted nothing more to do with him.

Focused on securing the gold independently, Veronica knew she had logistical hurdles to overcome. Given the gold's weight, she could carry only two bars at a time. She estimated there were over one hundred, so she'd need the right equipment to do the job. A quick Amazon search led her to rent a van to transport the gold; and order a lightweight 10-foot ConveyorEase conveyor belt for $2,599 to carry the gold; along with a Vevor Power Electric Hoist for just under $200 to lift it into the van. Yet, even with the right equipment, she realized she couldn't do this whole job alone. The only person she could think to trust was her middle son, Harry, so she gave him a call.

"Hello, Harry. I was wondering if I could come over to your place to have a discussion with you."

"Sure, Mom. I'd love to have you over for a talk. Come on over," Harry said.

When she arrived at his apartment, Veronica knocked on the door, and Harry opened it.

"Hi, Mom. I'm so glad you're here. I've really missed you. How are you?"

"Well, I have a special favor to ask of you, and I need to know if I can trust you with some sensitive information."

"Of course, Mom."

"Do you feel like you have to share everything with your brothers?"

"No, Mom. They haven't treated you fairly, so I don't think it's right to tell them everything if you ask me not to."

"I appreciate that, especially because this could benefit you."

"Really?"

"I need you to help me with something that's, well, kind of illegal."

"Mom, are you serious?"

"I need to explain this fully, and you'll have to believe me if you decide to go along with it. Your grandfather left us a fortune. It's buried beneath the old house in Tucson, and I know exactly where it is. I have all the tools we need to retrieve it. We can do this together, just you and I, and we'll be unimaginably wealthy. But we can't tell my sister; she'll take advantage of the situation and claim it all. The homeowner will try to do the same. The treasure belongs to us—it's the Lost Confederate Gold."

"Wait, what? I heard you've been saying some pretty outlandish things lately."

"You have to believe me; we'll be rich. Have I ever lied to you?"

"No, but you're getting older, and I'm just not sure..."

"Here's my offer: I'll lay out the whole plan for you and then provide proof of the gold's existence. If you're not convinced, we'll abandon the plan, and you can forget I ever mentioned it."

"That sounds fair, but I want to see the proof first."

"Alright, let's take a trip to Tucson."

"Okay."

They arrived in Tucson as darkness fell. Veronica directed her son to park at the Walco closest to her old neighborhood. She had advised him to dress in black, as she had done. She demonstrated how she could enter the basement undetected through the window well under the kitchen window. There was a window she could squeeze through, down into the planter shelf at the bottom, and then, jimmy the window lock open to the basement.

"The alarm system doesn't register down here due to the

concrete walls and lack of Wi-Fi. The McGregor family is on Long Island for another week, so now is the perfect time for this."

Veronica led him through a narrow hallway lined with empty bookcases that once held her father's treasured books. Their emptiness seemed to cast a shadow of sadness as if begging to be refilled. Even her son felt a cold shiver as they moved through the basement, as though the place itself was trying to communicate something. As they approached the wall, her son paused abruptly, looking unsettled.

"Are you okay?" Veronica asked.

"Yes, Mom. It's nothing, just my imagination," he replied.

""That may not be the case," she said cautiously.

""Oh, Mom, be realistic. I'm fine."

Veronica retrieved her tools from the satchel she'd been carrying and cut a small hole in the wall, large enough to insert an arm and feel for the gold bars.

"Now, put your hand in," she instructed her son.

"They are gold bars!" he exclaimed, pulling one out slowly. Each bar weighed nearly thirty pounds.

"We're going to be rich, Mom! How many do you think there are?"

"I estimated about 120," she answered.

"Hand me that bag of yours, and I'll carry two bars back to the car. When should we execute this plan?"

"We could do it tonight since everyone is still away," Veronica suggested.

"You've got all the equipment in the van, right? What's the plan?" Harry inquired.

"I bought a conveyor belt and a hoist," Veronica began. "We'll place the conveyor belt in the hallway, so we don't have to carry the bars far. We put them on the belt one at a time. Once all the bars are in the last room, the other person will go outside, back up the van, jimmy open the window above the basement planter, and lower a net attached to the hoist lever. Then, the person in the basement puts the bars into the net on the windowsill. When the net is full, the person in the van operates the electric hoist to lift the bars and directs the net into the back of the van. After that, we switch the nets and continue the process."

Veronica paused, catching her breath.

"We'll also need to restore the basement to its original condition to avoid detection. Security cameras could be a problem, but the only one we need to worry about is the one outside the kitchen. We'll take it down and disable it."

Exhausted, Veronica fell asleep during the drive back to Phoenix, her son at the wheel.

"Hey, where are we?" Veronica woke suddenly, as she felt the van come to a complete stop.

"We're at my place, Mom. Time to get some sleep," her son said. "But first, I have to ask you: How did you know about the gold? Will you tell me the truth? Why didn't you find out about it earlier, before you moved out or before Karina sold the house? And why doesn't Karina know about this?"

"I'm hesitant to tell you because I'm afraid you'll think I'm crazy. Let's just say your grandfather—"

"His ghost spoke to you?" her son interrupted.

"How did you know?"

"I saw him."

"Where?"

"At the house. He was pointing at you and saying 'Believe!'"

Veronica looked deeply into her son's eyes.

"He came back and told me about our family history. He urged me to keep it alive and specifically warned me not to trust Karina. According to him, she's not of our blood. This gold is the Lost Confederate Gold. We should donate it to the Smithsonian. We'll still become wealthy, but more importantly, our family will secure its place in history as it should."

"Does this mean I can see ghosts?"

"It suggests you might possess magical abilities you're not even aware of," Veronica replied.

"Your grandfather came back because of his untimely death.

There's so much to tell you. You might be the next generation of magic in this bloodline. Now I know I was right in trusting you. You've always had a special affinity for animals, like me. Things are becoming clearer now."

She chuckled softly.

Suddenly, Veronica's cell phone went off.

"It's the Police Chief. I'd better take it."

"Thank you, Chief, for the information."

"Your aunt was just arrested for your grandfather's murder. 'Someone' anonymously turned in a second "doctored" autopsy report, causing Dr. Reginald Smith to confess to document tampering, and the police reopened the case of my father's murder. My sister has been charged with murder for poisoning my father with an overdose of cyanide."

"Now I wonder who did that! How did you ever get ahold of that report?"

"It was the dogs. They sniffed it out in the old Tucson basement, when I asked them to look for evidence of your grandfather and wrongdoing, and they uncovered these records that Karina thought she had thrown out in the trash of the old house."

"That must be such a relief to see them reopen the case, and for Karina to be indicted. I knew there was something wrong about her."

"You know, it is. In fact, that's all I wanted- for justice to prevail!"

"Oh, Mom, do you ever turn off your teacher's voice?"

"Well, you know I've got the part down so well. Why stop now?"

They both laughed.

"I wanted to thank you for looking out for me. I should have listened to you about Robert. He did end up being no good."

Her son nodded in agreement.

"I've always felt that people come along and try to take advantage when they see someone who is alone."

"You are right about that. Sometimes it's the voice of the next generation that brings us clarity."

"Oh, Mom, sometimes you are just so philosophical."

"It's the teacher in me. Thanks for sticking by me, son."

"I'm always here for you, mom, just like you've always been there for me."

"You know, I think that's what my dad put me up to this for to show me how important family and legacy are. I don't want to take that away from you either. So I think we should keep this gold protected. And keep this legacy going through the ages. It has sustained our family. Sure, we can take a few bars to help get back our home, so the rest won't be lost, but the rest need to be sealed to be protected and passed on as a security blanket for our family. I think we should just take enough, maybe 5, to make up for the mistakes Karina made and help pay for the taxes, to keep this house and the Mexico house running, put it in a fund as my father did, and have it keep paying the bills, and the kids, for years to come. Then I can teach you the magic my father taught me, and you can keep that tradition going with your children."

"Wait. What children, Mom?"

"Well, when you have them, Harry." They both laughed.

"I guess I'd better get a girlfriend first."

"That's where some of this magic might give you some confidence in that area, so don't worry, Harry."

Together, they carefully planned their next steps, balancing the need for secrecy with the desire to right the wrongs of the past.

Back in Tucson, Veronica stood in the dimly lit basement, her hand trembling as she cut away the last part of the wall to the room filled with gold. But, as the piece of wall fell backward, there revealed not just the long-hidden treasure, but also a trove of old family documents. Veronica realized that these papers held real value, offering insight into her family's history and her father's life. It was a window to a past filled with love, sacrifice, and resilience —a past that shaped her identity.

The gold, while valuable, seemed insignificant compared to the newfound understanding of her heritage. Her father's voice echoed in her mind, "Wealth is not in gold, but in the stories we leave behind." It was this revelation that prompted Veronica to make a decisive choice.

She and Harry resealed the treasure chamber, leaving most of the gold untouched, and took only the documents, and five of the gold bars. It was a symbolic act, signifying her shift in values. Her treasure was her family's story, one she and Harry intended to preserve and pass on.

Veronica's return to the surface was not just a physical one; it was a metaphorical rise from the depths of uncertainty to a place of clarity and purpose. She knew her journey was not just about righting the wrongs of the past, but about shaping a future that honored her family's legacy.

The resolution of the mystery surrounding her father's death had brought her some needed closure, but it was her personal growth that marked the true climax of her story. She had evolved from a woman driven by vengeance to a guardian of her family's history, ready to face the future with a newfound sense of identity and purpose.

As Veronica sat down to write the story of her family, she felt a sense of peace. The journey had been challenging, filled with danger and betrayal, but it had led her to a deeper understanding of herself and her place in the world.

The final words of her manuscript read: "In the end, our true legacy is the story we write with our lives—a story of love, family, and the courage to right the wrongs in our lives."

With these words, Veronica closed her laptop, gazed out the window at the setting sun, and smiled. She was ready for whatever the next chapter of her life held.